46 HOURS TO HOME

A novel of survival during the apocalypse

Pat Riot

CONTENTS

Acknowledgements

When I first started this project I vastly underestimated the amount of time I would put into this book. Between the first outline, all the drafts, adding stuff and taking other stuff out, and the research, I estimate that I put several hundred hours into writing 46 Hours to Home. Of course something like this is never accomplished by just one person. To Cheryl: Thank you for your insights and help with proofreading. Your assistance was invaluable. To my brother: Thank you for all your help. With all the ideas and numerous hours reading the drafts, this book would not be what it is today without you. And most importantly, to my wife: from the bottom of my heart, thank you for believing in me, pushing me, keeping me level, and encouraging me; I am a better person because of you. You are the light of my life and I love you with all of me.

For those of you that take the time to read this book I say THANK YOU! I truly hope you love the book and come away wanting more. If you love it, like it, or even hate it, please take the time to rate it and leave some constructive feedback. I plan to keep writing and will hopefully improve as an author with your help. Enjoy.

PROLOGUE

93 million miles above earth the sun was in a period known as solar maximum with sunspot, solar flare, and coronal loop activity at increased levels. On March 25, just after 1:00 pm UTC the sun would explode into activity. On the earth facing side of the sun, in an area with an unusually high number of sunspots, a solar flare, later identified as a class X32 flare, would erupt and release a coronal mass ejection containing billions of tons of plasma aimed directly at earth. Due to the heightened solar activity, several smaller coronal mass ejections had already occurred over the prior several days, effectively clearing the area between the sun and earth of ambient solar wind plasma. Because of this, the massive coronal mass ejection caused by the class X32 solar flare would reach earth in under eighteen hours. While humans went about their daily lives sleeping, eating, working, texting on their cellphones, playing games and conducting meetings via the internet, driving cars and flying planes, the vast majority of earth's inhabitants had no idea the life giving sun would soon destroy modern civilization as we know it.

CHAPTER 1

"Control, Paul-38 on a traffic stop." Communications Supervisor Robert Miller used his computer mouse to deselect the channel covering the southwest area of the county, then used it to select the channel covering the northwest area without waiting to hear the expected response from the dispatcher working that radio channel. As he selected the new channel an officer yelling into his portable Motorola radio came through Rob's headset, "Charlie-14 PHYSICAL!"

He listened as Dispatcher Rachel Rodriguez went through the steps as laid out in the agencies policies and procedures. First, he heard a tone sent out on the channel to alert everyone listening that something important was happening, then he heard Rachel speak in a very fast but clear and concise voice, "All units 10-33 repeating 10-33 Charlie-14 physical at 15505 Ashwood units to respond code-3." She cleared the radio channel and initiated what was referred to as "emergency traffic" which would hopefully keep anyone not involved in the critical incident from transmitting and taking up precious air time, potentially preventing the officers involved from putting out critical information.

Rob continued to listen as numerous units responded to the call for urgent assistance from Charlie-14.

"Charlie-11 code 3" … "Charlie-23 rolling code" … "Charlie-20 en-route." The whole time he could hear Rachel typing furiously into the Computer Aided Dispatch system tracking everything that was going on with the speed and accuracy of a competent and well-trained dispatcher. Once she had a moment of free air time she activated her headset mic, "Northwest watch commander, copy?" A moment later Rob heard the sergeant currently acting as watch commander for that area respond, "Sam-5 I copy, show me responding."

As many times as Rob had been in that seat taking the radio traffic of an officer in distress, as many times as he had handled this same situation and even situations that resulted in officers being involved in a shooting, including officers taking fire from a suspect, he could still feel his heart speed up just a little. No matter the situation there was always a part of him that worried that the officer would be injured or worse. As much as he wanted to take over the channel from Rachel he knew she was a good dispatcher and didn't need any assistance with the radio traffic. Instead he called over to her, "I'll start medical for you".

"Copy!" Rachel replied as she continued to type.

He reached for a small keypad situated on the console in front of him and pushed the button labeled County Fire Dispatch, then listened to the line ring twice before being answered. "Hey this is Michelle," he heard the friendly voice of the county fire department's dispatcher come through his headset.

"Hey Michelle, can you guys start for 15505 Ashwood, we have a unit physical."

"No problem, we'll stage for you."

"Okay thanks," Rob said before hanging up and yelling over to the dispatcher assigned to the southwest command area radio channel, "Hey Tracy, start your K-9 unit up there in case they need it." Rob knew a police canine was a valuable tool that could help with anything from tracking down and apprehending suspects to locating evidence and missing children. He also knew the officers appreciated when dispatch took the initiative to respond resources that could assist without the officers needing to ask for it.

As he waited for any updates from Charlie-14, Rob checked his screens. Just because he had an officer in a physical confrontation in one area did not mean he wasn't still responsible for everything else going on in the county. He looked at the call screen to check on everything currently happening across their jurisdiction. Three domestic violence calls, one death investigation on a thirty-eight-year-old male who possibly overdosed on heroin or a similar opioid, four traffic collisions, one of which was considered major injury, twelve burglar alarm calls, one fight call at a bar, nine suspicious vehicle calls, one stabbing currently under investigation, one shooting call where the officers were still trying to locate one of the three victims who walked away from the scene prior to anyone arriving, one lost hiker that had a helicopter and volunteer search and rescue team on the way to look for, and twenty-seven assorted calls that were not in progress and still pending dispatch. *Not a bad night, all in all.* Next, he checked the screen that showed which officers were doing what along with their current location. Besides the officers on the calls currently dispatched he could see over seventy that were working special assignments, such as traffic enforcement, DUI patrol, surveillance on a few of the local gang bangers suspected of committing recent vehicle thefts, and the group of investigators currently in the next county over attempting to locate an assault-with-a-deadly-weapon suspect who had been on the run for over three weeks.

The next transmission to come through was from Charlie-14 and even though he was fighting with a suspect the officer's voice was composed and clear, "Control I'm still physical, Taser deployed but not effective. I've also got family coming out of the house." *Geez,* thought Rob, *this guy must be hopped on up something. And hopefully his backup units get there before the family decides to get involved.*

Fifteen seconds later the radio came alive again, "Charlie-23 and -20 both 97, -14 still physical keep the other units rolling."

"Copy -23 and -20 97, still physical, units remain 10-33," Rachel said into her mic while continuing to type.

"Sam-5 I'm about a minute out." Just over two minutes later he heard what everyone in the room was hoping, praying, and waiting to hear, "Sam-5 we are code four, one in custody, roll in medical for the suspect, all officers are code four. Send two additional units, we have a large crowd of family and neighbors semi-uncooperative."

Rachel responded, "10-4, Charlie-25 and -29 both respond. Medical is en-route."

Thank God, Rob thought with immense relief. The entire incident had lasted a little less than four minutes but felt like hours. It was a relief to hear that Charlie-14 was OK and the only person in need of medical aid was the suspect. There was a small part of him that was glad the suspect would be heading to the hospital prior to being taken to the county jail. *What's that saying?* Rob thought to himself. *Oh yeah, play stupid games, win stupid prizes. What an idiot.*

"Tracy, your K9 unit can cancel," Rob called out, then reached over and pressed the button to call County Fire Dispatch again. "This is Angie," he heard after one ring.

"Hey, it's Rob. Reference that call on Ashwood, you guys can roll in."

"Copy that," Angie responded. "Your officers okay?" she asked.

"Yeah they are. Just the suspect needs some tender loving care from the county's bravest," Rob joked.

"Okay you got it," Angie said with a laugh.

Rob disconnected the call then yelled over to the other side of the room, "Hey Rachel, good job as usual. You need a break or anything?"

"No, I'm good, thanks though. And thanks for getting medical for me," she replied.

"You're welcome," Rob said as he turned his attention back to the computer to finish working on the schedule for the up-coming month. He was interrupted again when he heard some-one walking up behind him. He turned and found his manager, Kristine Davis, approaching. She was a tall pretty black woman with a reputation of being a bit of a hard-ass, but in his own opinion she was actually a very good boss and was fair with her employees; she just tended to come down hard on dispatchers who weren't putting their full focus into their job. He took off his headset as Kristine asked, "Hey, which sergeant went to that unit physical?"

"Sam-5," Rob replied.

"Okay, I'll see if I can get the scoop," Kristine said. "And Rachel did a great job, as usual."

"Yeah," Rob said, chuckling. "Those were almost my exact words to her."

After a quick smile Kristine turned and walked back towards her office. Rob decided to take a break. Besides the officer who fought the suspect a minute ago there was nothing major cur-rently going on and the schedule could wait. He picked up his headset and pressed the button to dial the supervisor console in the other dispatch room.

"PSAP, Jason," the voice came through the headset. Jason Johnson was the supervisor overseeing PSAP, which stood for Public Safety Answering Point. It was the side of dispatch that took all incoming emergency and non-emergency phones calls from the public and other agencies. Most small to medium size agencies have both radio and PSAP in the same room, but due to the layout of the building they were in and the fact they were considered a large dispatch center, they were split into two separate but still large rooms. At any given time, there would be anywhere from twenty to thirty dispatchers working. Jason was new in the position, having been promoted a bare three months prior, but was quickly proving himself to be a well-liked and competent supervisor. In the seven years Jason was employed with the agency, he and Rob became good friends. They worked numerous shifts together and got along great, both having a somewhat immature sense of humor, laid back attitudes, and a friendly outlook on everything. Jason, like Rob, was quick to laugh but also knew when to take things seriously and worked hard when needed. Both were also known as good dispatchers who were now good supervisors, and everyone liked working on their shifts.

"Hey Jason, Rob, I'm gonna take a break, keep an eye on things?"

"Always, just let me know when you get back, I need to get some coffee" Jason said.

"Okay, will do."

After hanging up Rob stood up and looked out over the darkened room. The walls were painted a light gray and the ceiling lights were all on dimmers and divided into several different sections. Each section could be dimmed or brightened based on the dispatcher's preference. Right now, every section was as dim as the switch allowed without being completely turned off. Each console also had its own small lighting system so if one dispatcher liked the room dark, but another liked it bright, they could both adjust their own console, and both be happy. Besides the two supervisor consoles that were slightly elevated above the rest of the room, there were five pods of three consoles each, making fifteen positions that could be used to monitor and work the numerous different radio channels that the agency relied on to accomplish its public safety mission. Of the fifteen consoles nine of them were currently occupied with the dispatchers working anything from primary radio channels to backup and special request channels. Along the walls were numerous cabinets that held everything from printer paper to boxes of pens.

As he looked around the room Rob could see all five televisions that were mounted above the pods were tuned to different channels with three playing movies, one a home renovation show, and the last a cable news station, but the dispatchers had their full attention on their screens. Rob felt a touch of pride as he watched for a moment. He had a good group of people on his shift. They were always on time, took their job seriously, were all strong dispatchers, and didn't cause any issues. And, surprisingly, they all got along. There was usually one or two who for one reason or another disliked the other dispatchers on their given shift and made it well known, causing morale issues. But that was not currently the case and Rob counted himself lucky that he didn't have to deal with the many problems that typically resulted with dispatchers who had a less than desirable outlook on life.

Before walking away Rob took a quick look at the alarm panel that was supposed to sound an alert if any issues occurred with any of the many different systems that were used in the communications center every day and found all the system lights were showing green. He also looked at the large monitor mounted above the alarm panel that showed the status of the radio system, including each individual radio channel, and could see no alerts pending on it. Everything in the darkened room appeared to be operating like it should. Rob announced to the room, "Taking a quick break, Jason is in PSAP if you guys need anything, I'll be back in a few." He didn't bother waiting to hear if anyone responded, knowing they heard him but were concentrating on their duties.

He left the room and entered the hallway, walking towards the exit door and passing the break room, locker room, and conference room. The building was older, built in the 1960's, and made of cinderblock painted an off white with dark green trim. When the center was built the hill it sat on was selected not just for better radio coverage due to the elevation over the surrounding areas, but because it was secluded as well. That was no longer the case as neighborhoods were built up over the last couple decades and now surrounded the center. It had two levels, the one with the dispatch rooms, and a basement. The building also had numerous radio antennas of various types and several satellite dishes mounted on a large radio-tower that was installed on the middle of the roof.

When Rob walked through the exterior door he was surprised to find that it was already dark out. During late March in Riverside, California he knew the sun set sometime around 7:00 pm. As he walked into the rear parking lot, where they were lucky enough to have an outdoor patio break area set up, he checked his watch. 8:32 pm. *Dang,* he thought to himself. *I feel like I just got here. Time flies when you're having fun I guess.* He had started his shift at 2:00 pm on this cool spring day. As he walked into the break area he pulled out his cell phone and checked his text messages. He only had one, from his wife Monica, which read, "Hey vid chat me when you have a chance."

He pulled up the correct app on his cell phone and pressed his wife's picture to initiate the call. After some ringing the screen changed and a video feed of his wife sprang into view. *Damn she's beautiful*, he thought to himself, not for the first time. *How did I get so lucky?*

Monica was 26 years old, about five feet six inches tall, with dark brown eyes and dark brown hair. She had that perfect caramel skin that Rob loved so much, and she worked hard at staying in shape. After giving birth eleven months prior, she was back to her pre-pregnancy weight due to working out at least three times a week and eating mostly healthy. Monica was born and raised in the United states but was first generation American, her parents immigrating from Mexico several years before she was born. Her father passed away five years prior after a long battle with lung cancer and her mother moved back to Mexico shortly after her husband passed away so that she could live out her life on the ranch she grew up on.

"Hey babe," he heard from the phone.

"Hey gorgeous, how you guys doing?" he asked.

"Good. I just put Jackson in bed. He's already out, he had a fun day playing with his cousins. I'm just gonna finish cleaning up the kitchen and get some reading done for my class, then crash out myself. You still getting off on time?" Prior to giving birth Monica worked as an emergency medical technician in a level one trauma center at a hospital in the next county over. Once she gave birth she resigned her position to become a full-time mom. Fortunately, Rob brought home enough money to cover their expenses and it allowed Monica to concentrate fully on their son. However, being a registered nurse was something she always dreamed of and she was now taking classes at the local community college, working towards achieving that goal.

"So far it looks that way. I think Gloria from dayshift called out, but Kristine hasn't asked me to hold over yet, maybe she asked Jason." Rob worked twelve hour shifts but it wasn't uncommon to be asked to hold over to assist with staffing. Like most dispatch centers across the country, they suffered from chronic staffing issues. As much as he wanted to be home with his wife and son, they could also use the extra money, so he usually held over a couple times a week.

"Okay no worries," Monica said.

"What do you think about going to the beach on Wednesday?" Rob asked his wife.

Her eyes lit up. She loved the beach even more than Rob did. "Since when have I ever turned down the beach?" she asked the rhetorical question with a smile. "We just have to be back by five. I have class that night."

"Oh yeah, that's right," Rob said while mentally kicking himself for forgetting his wife's schedule. "We can leave for the beach early and come back early in the afternoon. Be home around two or so."

"Sounds like a perfect day to me."

"Yeah me too. And we'll go to that place for fish tacos on the way home."

"Yes!" He could tell Monica was excited now. "Okay babe, I'm going to go so I can get some studying done. Text me when you are on the way home, I'd hate to accidently shoot my husband thinking he was an intruder," she said with a mischievous smile.

"HA! Accidently my butt," he said sarcastically. *Damn, I love that smile.* "Get some rest babe, I'll see you in the morning, I love you more than anything. Give Jack a kiss goodnight for me."

"Okay Robby, drive home safe, love you too." She blew Rob a kiss prior to ending the video feed.

He checked his watch again. 8:36 pm. He had enough time to walk around the building a couple times. At some point in the past someone took the time to measure out the perimeter of the property the dispatch building was on and found that if one was to walk around it three times they had walked just under a mile. There was now a small walking trail that circled the property, made by numerous dispatchers walking numerous miles along the same path since the location was built. The path followed the back edge of the parking lot to the north side of the building where the agency's fleet services operated. This office of fleet services was where all the extra electronics, such as the radios and lightbars, were installed on new units and repaired when they broke on older units. Once the trail exited the back parking lot, where several dozen police units were parked waiting for service it, continued following the large fence, circling around until it met up with the parking lot at the front of the building. From there it went through the front parking lot and through a large grass area with several mature trees before swinging back around to the rear of the building and into the rear parking lot.

Rob was white, twenty-nine years old, five feet eleven inches, with brown eyes and a bald head he shaved almost daily; his thinking being once the hair starts going why not just help it along? He did his best to move around on his breaks, not so much to keep in shape, but to get his muscles moving and blood flowing. As a dispatcher, since his agency didn't utilize wireless headsets, he was literally tethered to his console while he was working and couldn't move around much during his shift, except for the short breaks he was able to take if nothing major was happening. He did make use of the gym that was set up in the building a few times a week to lift weights, but he hated doing cardio, which is why he was packing a few extra pounds. Last time he stepped on a scale he was pushing 200 pounds. He would much rather hike in the local hills around Yucaipa, the city he lived in, but didn't have much time for that lately with a newborn at home.

Rob passed the halfway mark on the walking trail and as he enjoyed the brisk night with stars in the clear sky his thoughts wandered to his extended family. Both his parents, one of his two brothers, and his sister all moved to Arizona a few years prior. They loved California but could no longer stomach the politics and how the state seemed to make things easier for criminals every time the politicians voted new laws into place. Between the gun control laws and criminal reform laws that were supposed to help reduce crime, but instead had the opposite effect, his family moved out of state and regularly encouraged Rob and his brother who still lived there to move to Arizona as well. *I wonder if Matt is working tonight?* Matthew was Rob's brother who still lived in California. He was single with no kids and lived in a small apartment not too far from Rob's house in Yucaipa. Because they were the last ones in the state, they were very close, and Matt was a great uncle to Jackson. Matt was also a police officer for the city of Redlands and worked crazy shifts and hours just like Rob did.

Rob made his lap around the property and marveled at all the upgrades that had been made to the aging building in the last few years. A little over a year after September 11, 2001 the Department of Homeland Security was created. One of the assignments they were tasked with was figuring out which public safety sites across the United States were considered high risk to terrorist attack and critical to assisting responding agencies in the event of an attack or natural disaster, then upgrading the security of that site. As the largest and main PSAP and radio dispatch facility in the county, the center was designated as high risk and critical for disaster response. DHS decided that the communications center needed to be hardened against a conventional terror attack and upgraded to withstand long term power outages. If this center was taken offline it would severely impede the ability of agencies to receive information from the public via 9-1-1 and to dispatch responding resources to a major disaster in the area. As such, DHS awarded grants to the agency to install what the employees took to calling the "Jurassic Park" fence that now encompassed the entire property. Prior to the upgrade the fence was simple chain link that only covered the rear parking lot, leaving the front half the of building exposed to anyone that approached. *Someone would have to be in a tank if they had any hope of getting through this twelve-foot high fence,* Rob thought. In addition to the fence, the old generator that would provide emergency power to the facility was replaced with a much larger one that doubled its power output. This would allow the center to still receive calls and utilize the radio and computer aided dispatch systems even during a prolonged power outage. All they would need to do was keep the fuel tank supplied with diesel.

As Rob walked back towards the large cinder block building he debated getting something to eat but decided to let Jason take a break and get coffee prior to taking care of his own hunger. Using his key-card to access the building through the rear door he re-entered the climate-controlled facility and made his way to the dimly lit PSAP room. This part of the center was larger than the radio side, housing twenty-seven consoles capable of receiving the one million plus 9-1-1 and other phone calls made annually by anyone within the agency's jurisdiction. The consoles here were set up the same as the radio side, three consoles to a pod, but with nine pods total instead of the five in the radio room, with TV's and the same system monitoring panel and monitor mounted on the walls.

"Hey Jason, how's it going in here?" Rob asked his colleague.

"Pretty good, not as busy as last night. Green Giant just called in," Jason said with a grin.

"No shit?" Rob laughed. "I haven't talked to him in quite a while."

"Apparently he's watching over northwest for us tonight."

"He ain't doing a very good job, he never showed up to Charlie-14's boxing match," Rob continued to laugh. Green Giant was someone who called in several times a week, always a few hours after sunset. While he had mental issues he was harmless, mentally living in an alternate reality where he believed he was a super hero known as Green Giant who assisted local law enforcement during the nighttime hours. The officers that knew him all said he was a nice guy who didn't create any problems, and since his once a night calls into dispatch were always short and harmless Rob didn't mind Green Giant calling in as he always caused amusement amongst the dispatchers. Unlike some of their other regulars who were regularly verbally abusive and did nothing more than tie up emergency lines.

"Yeah, I guess not," Jason said, then changed subjects. "I'm glad Charlie-14 is okay. I was listening in. I hope that dirt bag got what he deserved."

"Yeah no kidding."

Jason suddenly turned serious. "Hey, did you see that alert that came through on the fax?" he asked as he pulled a single sheet of paper from under his keyboard.

"No," Rob responded as he reached for the alert. "When did it come in?"

"About thirty minutes ago," Jason said. "It's not one I've ever seen before and I'm not sure what to make of it," Jason continued as he handed the fax to Rob.

As a public safety communications center, they received all types of alerts throughout the day, usually courtesy of the ancient technology of a fax machine, and sometimes through the state CLETS, or California Law Enforcement Telecommunications System, or the federal NLETS, or National Law Enforcement Telecommunications System. Usually the alerts were things like severe weather alerts issued by the National Weather Service, but also included Amber alerts, and any potential officer and public safety alerts issued by other local, state and federal agencies.

Space Weather Message Code: ALTK04
Serial Number: 2094
Issue Time: 2019 Mar 25 0510 UTC

ALERT: Geomagnetic K-index of 9

Threshold Reached: 2019 Mar 25 0759 UTC
Synoptic Period: 0700-1000 UTC

Active Warning: Yes

Major solar storm activity has been detected. Possible radio, telecommunication, and GPS interruptions. Be prepared for minor to moderate power grid fluctuations.

Potential Impacts: Area of impact primarily north of 15 degrees Geomagnetic Latitude.
Induced Currents - Major power grid fluctuations can occur.
Aurora - Aurora may be visible at low latitudes covering much of North America.

"I've seen this type of alert a couple times, but normally we receive it something like twenty-four to thirty-six hours before the event is supposed to affect us, not two hours. And I've never seen it say major solar storm like that. I think normally is says 'Solar Activity has been detected,' or something like that," Rob said as he contemplated the message. It gave him pause, but he didn't voice his concern as he wasn't exactly sure why the fax made him feel uneasy. "The couple times I've seen it nothing has happened, but I'll let you know if the radios start going down the toilet. Go take your break, I'll keep an eye on things."

"Okay cool, I'll let you know when I'm back," Jason said as he got up from his console.

As Rob made his way back over to radio he couldn't shake the bad feeling the alert had given him. Even though he kept running it through his head he couldn't figure out why it gave him an ominous feeling. When he walked into the radio room Kristine waved him over to her office. "Hey, you know who Charlie-14 is?" she asked as Rob walked through the doorway.

"No, I didn't bother to check."

"It's Sam Gutierrez."

"Really? Who would want to fight him? He's like a mini

version of The Hulk." Officer Sam Gutierrez was well known throughout the department. He spent at least one hour, and usually two or three, per day six days a week in the gym. He was only average height at five-six but very powerfully built. His arms were thicker than most guy's thighs and he prided himself as a boxer. Only someone truly desperate would decide to fight with him, and even then, they still had to know they were going to lose. There were several incidents in which Officer Gutierrez took down suspects who were at least six inches taller and outweighed him by fifty to one hundred pounds without breaking a sweat.

"Apparently the dirt bag is a PAL," Kristine said, using the acronym for Parolee at Large, someone who had violated the terms of their parole and were considered a fugitive. "He had a gun in his back pocket too. Gutierrez broke the guy's nose. And after they had him detained the guy's girlfriend came out of the house bleeding from her head saying he beat her down too."

"Wow," stated Rob. "I'm glad Gutierrez is okay. That guy is lucky he didn't get shot". To himself he thought, *no wonder the guy fought, parolee at large with a gun in his pocket having just beat up his girlfriend, he's definitely going back to prison. At least I hope, never know with the jacked-up justice system in California.* It was a huge relief to hear Gutierrez was fine. Rob only knew him in passing, meeting him only a couple times, so Rob didn't really know him personally, however like all Law Enforcement, there was a bond that came as a result of their shared responsibility of public safety.

"Yeah seriously," responded Kristine while shaking her head before changing the conversation. "Hey, are you done with that schedule yet?"

"Almost, another hour maybe."

"Okay, just forward it to me and the front office when you're done. They said they want to be included in that stuff. I'm not sure why, but we just do what we're told, right? Also, I'm leaving for the night, I'll be back tomorrow at 0800 hours for that budget meeting with the brass." Kristine shook her head and rolled her eyes when she mentioned the budget meeting.

"Better you than me," Rob said with a smile. The budget meetings were usually very tedious, with all the division heads crying wolf over perceived lack of funding and begging for extra money to be set aside for projects they always deemed critical to the agency, even though to Rob the special projects almost always sounded like a ridiculous waste of resources.

"I'll be sure to get you assigned to it for next year then. Now get outta my office." Kristine had a serious look, but Rob knew she was joking with him.

"Yes ma'am," he said with sarcasm. "Have a good night, I'll see you on Thursday."

"You too," she replied, finally smiling.

He left Kristine's office and went back to his console to finish the schedule. When he sat down Rob started thinking about what occurred earlier with Officer Gutierrez and that led to thoughts of the single most traumatic incident he had been a part of as a dispatcher.

He was assigned to work the radio channel for the central division of the county. It was late, after 10:00 pm, and there was not much going on that Tuesday night. Even for a weekday night it was quieter than normal. Rob received a call on his CAD screen for a noise complaint about someone sitting in a car in their own driveway playing loud music from the car radio. Rob assigned the call to the officer working that beat and due to nothing else going on the response time was less than ten minutes. After going on scene, the officer requested a unit to back him up due to an uncooperative subject and several family members coming out of the house. Several more officers responded but the closest one was about ten minutes away. A few minutes later the officer that was on scene keyed up his radio, but the only thing Rob could hear was what sounded like a struggle. Rob told the officer he couldn't copy the radio traffic and asked him to repeat it. The officer keyed up again and this time Rob could hear someone scream in the background. Numerous units responded code-3 but because the neighborhood was in a semi-rural area the first backup officer didn't arrive for almost eight minutes. During that time the radio belonging to the officer on scene kept keying up with sounds of a struggle and people screaming and yelling coming through.

When the first backing officer arrived, he transmitted the words no one in Law Enforcement ever wants to hear: officer down. In the next seventeen minutes over fifty additional officers from several different agencies arrived to assist. Later Rob would find out that when the initial officer arrived on scene he found a male inside the vehicle where the loud music was coming from. The male had been using a cocktail of different drugs and was not in his right mind and as the officer tried to speak to the male he got out of the vehicle and tried to walk away. When the officer attempted to detain him, the male resisted, and the officer took him to the ground. This is when the male's family came out of the house and jumped the officer. They beat the officer for several minutes before retreating into the house, taking the now unconscious officer's gun from his duty belt and leaving him lying on the ground in the driveway.

The officer was transported via helicopter to the closest trauma center where he held on for two more hours, enough time for his wife to be picked up and driven there by one of his partners so she could say goodbye, before succumbing to the massive head injuries he had been subjected to. It took a SWAT team six hours to convince the suspects to surrender. When it was all said and done five family members were charged with murder of a peace officer, but more importantly a wife was left without her husband, two children were left without their father, and a department was left without their brother. That night would be seared into Rob's memory for the rest of his life and it was something he would never truly get over, even after taking a week off and several sessions with the agency's psychiatrist. He used that night as an example to newer dispatchers to never become complacent in their jobs. Something as simple as a loud music call could result in the death of an officer.

Fifteen minutes later Jason walked in holding a spill proof tumbler full of coffee. "Hey thanks for covering, there's more coffee in there if you want it, I made plenty," he said to Rob.

"Is it that stuff your parents brought home from Hawaii?" Rob asked, hopeful that it was.

"Heck no, that stuff is off limits to savages like you. It's for us civilized folk only," Jason deadpanned.

"Savage? I'm the most cultured dispatcher you ever met. In fact, I've been to two whole other states and Mexico. And yes, Tijuana counts." Rob said with his best poker face.

"See? You think going to Las Vegas is visiting the state of Nevada, and Arizona barely counts. And no, Tijuana doesn't count. Ask your wife, she's been to real Mexico several times and she'll tell you. That's why you get the cheap coffee."

They stared at each other for a few seconds, waiting to see which one would break first. It was Rob. He burst into laughter, "Okay you got me, I'm uncultured swine. One day I will be as worldly as you, the guy who's never even been to Vegas."

Now Jason was laughing, "Yeah, yeah, yeah. Go get your coffee. Maybe the dirt water will help you out mentally."

"I'll get some in a few minutes. I need to take my lunch too."

"Okay no problem, I'll cover you. Hey while I was waiting for the coffee to brew I took a walk through the building. That side exit door from the basement that goes up to the side driveway?" Rob nodded. "It was standing open. You know if IT was supposed to be here tonight?"

"No, not that I know of. They are supposed to let us know, and I have nothing in my emails. Was it propped open?" Rob was puzzled. Everyone who worked in the basement worked eight to five and anytime they were there after hours they were supposed to let the on-duty dispatch supervisor know someone would be down there. Usually they only came in after hours if they were working on a technical emergency or if they were doing upgrades or updates to the systems that were best done after hours during times of lower radio traffic and phone call volumes.

"Not propped open, just standing open."

"That's weird. All the exterior doors have those automatic arm closer things at the top. None of them are supposed to be open. Let's go take a look." Rob stood up and addressed the room. "Jason and I are going to go check something out. I have my radio. If you guys need anything, I'll be on blue," Rob said, letting his people know which channel to raise him on if needed. He picked up the portable radio from the console, turned it on and made sure it was tuned to the correct channel, then looked at Jason and said, "Lead the way."

Both supervisors left the radio room and walked into the hallway. They went down about midway then turned into a stairwell and descended the flight of stairs into the dark basement. As they passed the door at the bottom of the stairs and entered the large basement, Jason reached over and flipped the switch for the overhead fluorescent lighting. Light flooded the basement, dim at first but growing steadily brighter as the bulbs warmed up. The large room was a combination office, server area for the computer and phone systems, and storage area. There were several cubicles that were used by the IT employees, several racks of phone switches, servers, and other computer equipment, and large metal shelves lining three of the walls filled with everything from extra headsets and chairs to fans and emergency disaster supplies.

After navigating the maze created by everything that was in the basement, they arrived at the still open door. "I didn't want to close it, I wasn't sure if someone was supposed to be down here. So, I decided to ask you first," Jason said.

"Yeah no worries. If they're here, then they broke protocol by not letting us know. They know how serious admin takes building security." Rob pulled the door closed. When he let go it started slowly swinging open again. "What the hell?" He closed it again, and again the door started opening. He stepped through the door and into the exterior stairwell. The stairs would take anyone who ascended them up to the side of the building and let them out onto the driveway that partially circled the building. When he took a closer look, he noticed something wrong with the latch that held the door closed. It was still recessed into the door. Rob pushed down on the lever type door knob and noticed the handle turned freely in the door. "Something inside must have broken. But the arm on top should have kept it closed."

Rob turned his attention to the top of the door and found someone had disconnected the arm. "What the...?" He trailed off as he thought about what he was looking at. Probably so they could leave the door open during the day for fresh air, someone disconnected the arm instead of using something to prop the door open. "The latch being broken is easily explainable. The building is older than both of us, and stuff happens. But the arm being disconnected? Heads are going to roll when Captain Jones hears about this."

"That's for sure," Jason agreed. "I'm glad I'm not going to be on the receiving end of that ass chewing." The captain had a well-deserved reputation for being a by the book administrator and was known to come down hard on anyone that did not follow policies and procedures. Rob found it somewhat fascinating, as the captain wasn't a screamer, but had a knack for making one feel as if their minor screw up was the end of the world. There were few people that could make someone wonder if their job was on the line just by giving them a certain look and Captain Jones was certainly one of them. "You want to write this up?" Jason continued. "Or you want me to do it?"

"You ever done one?" Rob asked as he reached up and reconnected the arm.

"No."

"There's a form in the computer, I'll show you where it's at. Write it up and I'll take a look at it then have you submit it. It'll be good training for you."

"Sounds good to me," Jason said.

Once the door arm was reattached Rob made sure it was functioning properly. Unfortunately, with the latch broken the door would remain unsecure, something that was not supposed to happen and was frowned upon by the higher ups. There were several past incidents where unknown people tried to gain access to the property and officers had to respond in from the field to detain them and figure out who they were. Most of the time they turned out to be people with mental issues or people who were just lost and needing directions, but in the age of terror threats and attacks, every incident and security breach was taken seriously and investigated fully. At least the reattached arm would hold the door closed now. "When you get back to your console make sure you have the camera that shows the outside stairwell, I think it's number twelve or thirteen, up on the security camera screen and just keep an eye on it. I'm sure building maintenance will be here first thing in the morning to get the latch fixed." Rob took one last look at the door. "That's as good as it gets. Let's head back up."

They retraced their steps back to dispatch and Rob followed Jason into the PSAP room where Rob showed him on the computer where the correct form was. "Let me know when you're done and I'll check it for you. I'll let the dispatchers know about the door."

When Rob was back at his console he sent out a mass message via the CAD system to the dispatchers currently working: "The basement exit door leading to the outside stairwell is broken. It's closed but not latched. As usual, if you see anyone you don't recognize on or around the property let myself and Jason know ASAP. If you use that door to exit for some reason, please make sure it shuts behind you. Thanks everyone."

Ten minutes later, as Rob was double checking the finalized schedule, he received a message from Jason: "Form is done. Ready for you to look at it when you have a chance." Rob didn't bother replying and instead got up and walked over to the PSAP room. When he arrived, Jason leaned to the side so Rob could get a better look at the screen.

"Looks good to me, just add in the time you found the door open and the time we went down there and tried to secure it. Also, in the miscellaneous section put that you monitored the stairwell using the security cameras. That will make sure we are covered. Then send it to Kristine and CC myself and the front office. Kristine will forward it up the chain and the front office will get maintenance on it first thing."

"Got it, thanks man," Jason said.

"No problem at all," Rob replied. "Hey, I'm going to eat. I'll let you know when I'm back."

Jason gave Rob a thumbs-up and Rob left the PSAP room. He walked into the break room, pulled out his lunch bag from the refrigerator, and sat down at the large table in the center of the room. As he ate he thought about his family. He thought about his son Jackson who was starting to walk. Not very far, just a few steps before falling onto his bottom. Watching Jackson grow and discover things and figure out how to do things was one of the most awesome things Rob would ever experience and thinking about it always made him swell with pride. In his own eyes Jackson was the most handsome and the smartest kid he ever had the privilege of laying eyes on. *Biased I know, but who cares? He's my kid, and he's amazing.* He thought of Monica and how she had adapted to motherhood with no problem at all. *She's a natural. She's going to make a great nurse. I sure picked a good one to spend the rest of my life with. Or, more accurately, I got lucky she let me choose her. Either way, asking her to marry me was the best decision of my life.* As he day dreamed he thought, not for the first time, *I would do anything to keep them safe and happy. Life is good.*

His thoughts turned to the space weather alert they received earlier. *It's gotta be a false alarm, right? We've received those before and they turn out to be nothing. Would the feds even warn us if they knew something bad was going to happen? Or would they be the usual slow federal government that takes months to decide on stuff that should be a no brainer easy decision?* Rob finished his lunch, cleaned up his small mess, then picked up his lunch bag, left the building, and walked to his truck. He left the bag on the hood of the truck next to the windshield on the driver's side and walked back towards the building. As he did, he thought, *No, it has to be an overreaction. The feds wouldn't tell us that something bad was coming. They would be too busy trying to cover their own asses and get themselves to safety, rather than admit to anyone that they were powerless to stop what was coming. And why can't I figure out why it's giving me a bad vibe?* If Rob knew how wrong he was about the federal government's response to what was coming, he would have gotten into his truck right then and drove home as fast as it would carry him.

Thousands of miles above the earth the coronal mass ejection, traveling at over one thousand miles per hour for almost eighteen hours, had entered the planet's exosphere and was already damaging satellites. The cloud of plasma, made up of electrons, protons, heavy nuclei, and magnetic field, was now slamming into the ionosphere and causing a geomagnetic storm that would wreak havoc on the magnetosphere. The resultant energy release would be measured on the petawatt scale and would cause the single most civilization changing event humanity had ever witnessed.

CHAPTER 2

Rob looked at the clock in the lower right corner of one of the five computer screens mounted in front of him. 11:18 pm. Just a few more hours and he would be on the way home. He was looking forward to having three days off with no overtime scheduled and was starting to think about the beach day he and Monica would enjoy a few days later. There was nothing like some "wave therapy" as he liked to call it. Rob wasn't a surfer or even a big swimmer, but there was nothing like sitting on the beach doing nothing else but listening to the break of the waves and feeling the ocean breeze on your face as you relaxed and forgot about the crazy world.

Working in this field, it was important to figure out at least one way to unwind and relax on your days off. If you didn't you could quickly find yourself in a downward spiral mentally and emotionally due to the traumatic incidents you experienced on an almost daily basis while taking 9-1-1 calls and dispatching officers to horrible situations. It could be psychologically damaging to sit on the phone with a screaming parent while their child stopped breathing, trying to coach them through CPR while medics responded, or talk to someone who's loved one was just ran over by a car.

One of the worst calls Rob remembered taking was from a fourteen-year-old boy. His sixteen-year-old brother was on the front stoop of their apartment when two men walked up and started asking the brother questions. For some reason they decided they didn't like the answers the brother gave and started yelling at him. The fourteen-year-old caller looked out the front window just in time to watch one of the suspects pull out a sawed-off shotgun from under his jacket, put it up against his brother's forehead, and pull the trigger. Rob would remember that call for the rest of his life. He would remember the disbelief in the caller's voice as he tried to give their address, the anguish in his mother's cries as she realized her oldest son was dead, the screaming of his father as he vowed revenge on the monsters who committed the crime, and the way the caller stopped answering questions. Rob later found out the kid went into shock and just stood and stared at his brother's lifeless body, now missing half its head, until the police and paramedics went on scene, then he broke down and cried for several hours when it finally hit him that his big brother was now dead. Rob was sure the kid would have nightmares for years and need lifelong therapy after witnessing something like that.

There is a saying amongst dispatchers: *No one calls 9-1-1 because they are having a good day.* There have even been several recent studies that showed dispatchers have a high rate of undiagnosed PTSD, especially since dispatch tends to be the forgotten aspect of first responders when it comes to public recognition. Rob was lucky that he had a wife that understood the stress he went through on a daily basis and did her best to help keep his head on straight.

As Rob sat looking at his screens he suddenly heard a loud pitched warbling type sound. The NAWAS phone was ringing. The National Warning Service was set up so that the federal and state governments could send out urgent alerts to first responder agencies that would be responding to disasters. It was meant for time critical alerts that the issuing agency felt shouldn't be delayed by the normal fax system that was utilized. Normally what Rob heard on the NAWAS was tsunami warnings, typically after a large earthquake occurred on the other side of the Pacific Ocean or up near Alaska.

Due to Riverside County being inland, the alerts normally

weren't meant for his center. How it usually happened is the phone would ring and out of the speaker a voice would announce who was issuing the alert, then list off the agencies the alert was meant for. If your agency was announced, you acknowledged the roll call, waited for the critical alert to come across, acknowledged that you copied the alert, then decided on a course of action based on the information received. However today the voice on the other end sounded a little rushed and stated: "Warning Center to all centers, standby for a critical alert..." This got Rob's attention. He grabbed a pen and notepad and got ready to write. The other unusual thing that happened was that the Warning Center didn't conduct the usual roll call. They usually made sure each agency that the alert was meant for was ready to receive information, but the voice just kept talking. "... earlier today the National Oceanic and Atmospheric Administration, along with NASA and the US Air Force, detected a major solar event occurring. They have advised that this event could affect telecommunications, GPS and power grid in your area of responsibility. All centers need to be prepared for possible power outages and telecommunications disruptions in their area of responsibility. The Warning Center will provide more information as needed." The voice then started to repeat the message.

What the hell? What does that even mean? And why was there so much static in the transmission? The Warning Center has always come through clear as a bell. That was really strange, Rob thought as he stood up and stretched his back as much as he could in the limited space behind his console. Then the faxed alert Jason handed him earlier came back to him. *There are one of two explanations for all this,* he decided. *Either the feds are overacting, and this really is nothing more than a somewhat stronger than typical solar storm, or they know it's going to be bad and aren't really saying, thinking they are going to stop a mass panic by the first responder community. Better safe than sorry though,* he decided as he pulled out his cell phone. He sent a quick text to his wife,

"Babe we got a couple weird alerts here at work, make sure you know where the candles and stuff are and keep a flashlight handy. Love you guys."

He turned away from the console and went over to the small restroom just outside the dispatch room in the hallway. As he was relieving himself and trying to decide how he should push the information out to the field units he felt his phone vibrate in his pocket. After he washed his hands and was walking out of the bathroom he pulled his phone out and found a reply text from his wife. "OK, don't worry about us. Having trouble sleeping but just took some melatonin, love you too." He would still worry no matter how much she reassured him she and their son would be fine.

As he walked back up to his console he decided it was better to put the information out via a message on the CAD system instead of a radio broadcast made by each dispatcher. When he arrived back at his console he reached down, grabbed the computer mouse and started to navigate around the CAD screen, selecting the messaging screen and checking the boxes for everyone the message would need to be sent to.

Rob was navigating around the screens when Rachel yelled out, "Hey Rob, my channel just went to shit. Everything is being drowned out with static."

He was about to ask the other dispatchers if they were also having radio issues when everything suddenly went black. All five computer screens, the portable Motorola radio sitting on the console in front of him, the overhead fluorescent lights, the small telescoping desk lamp over his keyboard, the five TV's mounted on the walls, even the alarm panel. All of it. One second it was on and working, the next it was all dead. Like someone had flipped the main breaker. Since the room had no windows at all it was pitch black. Not that they would have helped; it was dark outside.

Rob's first thought, *Okay, let's wait a second for the generator to kick in*, was followed quickly by his second thought, *why didn't the UPS system work?* The uninterrupted power supply system was basically a series of battery backups that were designed to keep power going to the computers and radios in the event of a complete power loss. They were rated to provide power for about fifteen minutes to all critical systems, so they should not have had any problem keeping the computers powered until the generator had time to start up and start supplying power to the building, which usually took about twenty to thirty seconds. Then Rob saw some lights turn on from the door that led out to the hallway and in the corner of the room. He realized it was the backup emergency lighting. They were battery powered and designed to only start up in the event of a power loss and if the generator failed to start up. He looked at the wall where the alarm panel was located. No lights anywhere. The panel had its own backup power supply and with the power being out the panel should have been showing several red indicator lights and sounding its high pitched alarm.

Rob stood up. "Anyone have any power on anything on their console?" He waited a few seconds and heard a smattering of "No's" and "Not here's." As his mind started putting everything together he went cold. *The faxed alert. The NAWAS alert. And now nothing is working. Holy shit, it can't be possible. I need to make sure before I do anything.* "Okay, everyone stay put, grab your emergency flashlights from under the console and then try to power on your backup radios, I'm gonna go out back and see if the generator is even running."

Even as he grabbed the emergency flashlight that was mounted under the console and turned to walk out Rob knew it was futile to check the generator. A couple years prior he was assigned to attend a training class that was based on terrorism but focused on a dispatch centers response to different types of attacks. One of the sections that the instructor briefly touched on was what was known as an EMP, or electromagnetic pulse. While Rob couldn't recall all the details, he did remember the instructor explained that if a nuclear device was detonated somewhere in the atmosphere it created this EMP that wreaked havoc on all things electronic. The instructor also said that a very large solar flare produced by the sun, if it hit earth, would have the same results.

After the class Rob was intrigued and did some research online on his own time. He found that if something like that occurred, and if it was large enough, it would knock the affected area back into the stone-age. He also read that while the government was aware of the issue, they were doing almost nothing to protect against such an event. What really got Rob was that a large solar flare had occurred in 1859. It was referred to as the Carrington Event, after the English astronomer Richard Carrington who recorded it. When the Coronal Mass Ejection that was produced by the solar flare hit earth, it produced auroras that were seen as far south as the Caribbean in the northern hemisphere and as far north as Columbia in the southern hemisphere. It also produced a massive EMP that melted telegraph cable lines and caused some operator's telegraph equipment to throw sparks. Since then there have been recorded CME's that have knocked out power to large areas and as recently as 2012 a "Carrington-class" solar storm missed earth by a mere nine days. Due to mankind's dependence on all things electric, including the internet, if a "Carrington-class" event occurred today and was to strike earth, it would literally be the end of the world as we know it. Some estimates put the loss of human life in the billions, maybe as much as ninety percent of the world's population perishing, if it were to ever occur, due to the dependence of humankind on electricity and the difficulty with producing and replacing damaged components in the system.

All of this ran through his mind as Rob made his way from the building into the rear parking lot. As he stepped out of the building exit door into the rear parking lot he stopped in his tracks. What caused him to stop was something that that he had never personally witnessed but was on his bucket list. It was an aurora and it was one of the most beautiful things he had ever seen. He paused for a good minute and stared in awe at the wondrous streaks of greens, purples, and oranges that made up light show.

He finally shook himself into action and jogged down the back side of the building then across the parking lot to the massive black and brown colored generator. He hit the button on the side that would normally activate a display that was supposed to show the current status of the generator (ready, not ready, fuel low, etc.) but nothing happened. It confirmed what he already knew: the almost brand-new generator was dead as well. As he walked back towards the building he realized there were no lights anywhere.

The dispatch center was built at the top of a hill and actually had good views of the city lights from the parking lots, but tonight everything except the sky was black. The surrounding neighborhoods were all relatively newer with large houses on large properties. All the houses were valued approaching one million dollars, with several being well north of that figure. All the houses were well taken care of with exquisite landscaping which included lighting systems in the yards that provided ambient lighting throughout the nights. Not being able to see any lights in the area was unsettling. "This is not good," he muttered to himself as he took out his phone. "This is actually very, very bad," he continued when his phone wouldn't turn on. Rob knew the charge was about fifty percent, but the screen wouldn't turn on. He long pressed the power button hoping beyond hope that it would power up, even though he already knew it wouldn't. Sure enough, it was as dead as the generator. He became more and more concerned and his despair grew as he put the phone back into his pocket and thought about everything that was happening.

The power was out, not just for the dispatch center but the city, the backup UPS systems did not work, the alarm panel that had its own backup power source was out, and the generator was dead along with his cell phone. Rob could only come up with one conclusion: an EMP had occurred and rendered the power grid and all electronics completely useless. He was convinced. *I need to get with Jason and come up with a plan, then get everyone moving. There is no point in staying here. The power is likely to be out for a very, very long time and things are going to go to hell. Depending on how wide spread this is, it could very well be every man for himself with complete anarchy before long. I have to get home to Monica and Jackson.* He closed his eyes for a moment and breathed deeply. Once he felt a little better he took the worry and despair and turned it into determination and focused on his ultimate goal. *I will get home to them, no matter who or what stands in my way.*

Rob made his way to the back door of the facility. Without thinking he put his key card up to the card reader to unlock the door. He shook his head at himself when he realized it wasn't going to work and tried to pull the door open. Locked. Of course, the power was out, it would have to be manually unlocked. Not thinking to use his building keys, he pounded on the door and a few seconds later it was opened by Jason who was also carrying an emergency flashlight.

"Hey man, generator out too?"

"Yeah, completely. All the lights in the city are out..." Rob trailed off as he realized Jason wasn't paying attention to him and instead was staring at the sky. It took Rob a second to realize Jason was looking at the aurora. He gave Jason a few moments to admire the beauty before getting his attention again. "Anyways yeah, the generator is out, and the entire city is blacked out too."

Jason blinked a couple times before he realized his mind had drifted off. "Sorry man, I've just never seen anything like it."

"No worries, I had the same reaction when I first came out. Enjoy it while you can, we'll probably never see anything like this again."

"Hey, you remember that training class they sent us to a couple years ago, the terrorism one with that tall skinny instructor from DHS?" Jason asked, now fully focused on Rob and speaking quickly.

"Yeah."

"This remind you of anything he said?"

"The EMP."

"Exactly," Jason agreed. "That's gotta be it right? I mean what else could cause this? Our backup systems have backups and the only thing that worked right were most of the emergency lights."

"Yeah man I know, we gotta decide what we are going to do. Let's take a quick walk around the building while we chat."

Jason followed Rob out into the parking lot and fell into step next to him. "What's up?"

Rob began, "Well, as I see it, this can't be anything else, or at least anything I've ever heard of. Power is out inside, generator is dead, its obvious power is out in the city, not to mention this aurora," Rob pointed towards the south where they could normally see miles of suburban city lights then pointed towards the sky. "So, hear me out." Jason just nodded. "With all of that, and remembering what that instructor said, I really think the shit has hit the fan then sprayed the entire room."

"Yeah, I'm with you so far, keep going," Jason said.

"Okay, everything that uses electricity is down, we have no

way to fix it, we have no way to do our job, and the way I see it nothing is going to be coming back to normal anytime soon. After we took that class I did some research online on my own and I found that if something like this happened it could take years for the power to be fixed. If that's the case, things are only going to get worse before it gets better. And I think it's going to get way, way worse. In that case I'm gonna be trying to get home. There isn't any point of staying here hoping the power comes back on."

"Yeah, but what if it does come back on?" Jason countered with concern in his voice. "What if you take off and a couple hours later it all starts working again?"

"I think I have to take that risk," Rob said quietly. "Besides, you try your cell phone?"

Jason took it out of his pocket and touched the screen. "Nothing."

At this point they were on the northeast side of the building, almost exact opposite of where they had started. "Look," Rob said as he swept his hand along the horizon. "The blackout is everywhere. There are no lights anywhere. You have your car keys?"

Jason patted his pocket, "Yeah, right here."

"Let's go try your car."

As they made their way back to the parking lot they both continued to admire the aurora, but this time Jason's awe was covered in a blanket of worry and Rob's awe was replaced with determination. Both could play devil's advocate and make counter arguments as to why the power outage had nothing to do with an EMP or solar flare, but they both knew deep down there was no other explanation.

Once they arrived at the rear parking lot Jason walked up to his silver Honda Civic and tried to use the key fob to unlock the doors. Nothing. He used the key to unlock the driver door and when he opened it the interior light came on. He immediately looked at Rob with a puzzled look on his face, "Why would the light turn on, but the key fob not work?"

Rob shrugged, "I have no clue, try to start it."

Jason did so. When he turned the key, there was no response. No slow crank of the engine, no clicking sound indicating it was trying to start, nothing. Jason turned on the headlights and they came on nice and bright. "See? I just don't get why the lights would work but nothing else."

"Me either, but let's think about what we have. Power is out everywhere we can see. The aurora. The generator, that's almost brand new and has never failed to kick on before by the way, is dead." The generator was tested monthly and had always performed flawlessly. "Your car doesn't start even though it's only a few months old. Hell, you just put the real plates on it's so new. Neither of our phones will even turn on even though they were both in perfect working condition thirty minutes ago. The backup systems never came on like they should have. Nothing. What else could it be?"

Jason stood outside his driver door for about a minute. Rob could see the wheels in Jason's head spinning so he stayed quiet. "Yeah, you're right. I keep trying to come up with some other reason why this could all be happening, but I just can't." Another quiet pause then, "Okay, I'm convinced. So, what do we do next?"

Before he could reply a loud explosion from the southeast caught their attention, followed by an orange glow just over the horizon. They both spun around but due to the terrain couldn't see anything. "C'mon!" Rob yelled as he turned and ran for the building, Jason right on his heels.

They made it to the backdoor in record time and Rob started to pound on it when Jason interrupted him, "Hold up, move, I got my keys."

"Ah! I'm an idiot, I didn't even think to use mine," Rob said with a disgusted shake of his head. Jason got the door open and they both ran into the building. When they made the turn into the hallways they almost ran into Rachel and three other dispatchers.

"Whoa! Watch it guys! In a hurry much?" Rachel asked, sounding irritated.

Rob didn't answer as he brushed by her and ran down the hallway. He reached the storage room at the end and used his master key to open it up while Jason used his flashlight to light up the door. Rob pushed open the door and went to the back corner of the 10 feet by 15 feet room where a ladder was built into the wall and went up into the ceiling, disappearing into the darkness. Rob started climbing and by the time he was half way up Jason was using his flashlight to light the way. Rob arrived at the top and turned a knob that unlatched the roof access hatch, used his arm and shoulder to shove it up and out of the way, then scrambled out onto the roof and made his way over to the southeast corner of the building, being careful not to trip on or run into any of the pipes, satellite dishes, antennas, and other equipment that crisscrossed the roof. He could see the fire before he reached the edge of the building. He heard several footsteps and with a quick glance over his shoulder realized Jason and the other dispatchers had followed him onto the roof.

"What is that?" Jason asked.

"I don't know one hundred percent, but I'm pretty sure that's a plane crash," replied Rob.

"Plane crash?" Someone, Rob wasn't sure who, asked with confusion in their voice.

"Yeah think about it. What's over in that direction a few miles?" Rob asked the group.

Jason was the first to make the connection, "March."

He was referring to March Air Reserve base. It was an active Air Force Reserve base and the dispatchers could regularly see military C-17 cargo planes fly in and out of the airfield.

"Exactly," Rob said. "Not only does the military fly out of their regularly but I'm pretty sure DHL, that package carrier, flies out of their too."

"Shouldn't we do something?" someone else asked.

"Like what?" Rob responded. "Normally we would pick up the phone or get on the radio and send help. But nothing works, so we can't do that. We could walk the few miles over there, but what would we do when we got there? We have nothing we can use to fight a fire like that and no real medical equipment other than the small first aid kits in the dispatch rooms. It sucks, but there is nothing we can do." Everyone grew quiet, thrown into a somber mood as the gravity of the situation started to really sink in on everyone present.

Rob watched the glowing fire for a minute or so while he thought over what he should do next. The obvious answer was to get home, but that was the overall goal. What should he do right now in this moment? His mind made up he turned to the small handful of dispatchers. "Okay listen up everyone. Head back inside, watch your step and don't fall down the ladder when you do, and gather everyone up. Emergency meeting in the rear parking lot, five minutes." Everyone could hear the seriousness in his voice and no one questioned him or hesitated to move towards the roof hatch.

As they walked towards the hatch Jason asked him, "What do you have in mind?"

"You'll see. I'm going tell everyone what we think is going on. The good thing is most of them have taken that same class at some point, so they should have at least a vague idea of we're talking about. Then, I'm headed home."

In silence they both walked back to the roof hatch, climbed down the ladder, and walked through the hallway and out the backdoor, which Rob propped open using a trashcan that was just outside. They walked over to the patio, where they stood in silence with their own thoughts while the shift of twenty-two dispatchers made their way out of the building and gathered in the patio area.

Once it appeared as if everyone was present, he did a quick head count to confirm, then stood on one of the patio chairs. "Okay everyone, quiet down. Who all took that terrorism class in the last two years, the one where they made dispatch a focus and taught us how to appropriately respond to different types of terror attacks?" About forty percent of the dispatchers raised their hands. "Good. Out of you that took the class, who remembers the part about the nuclear device or the solar flare wreaking havoc on the power grid and anything electronic?" Almost all the same hands went up again. "Okay. Well, I think that's what we have here. I don't remember all of the specifics, I don't know the science behind it, but I'm almost one hundred percent sure that's the cause of all this power loss."

"What are you getting at Rob?" The question came from the back of the crowd.

"Take a look around." He waited a moment while everyone looked around. "Notice anything strange?"

"All the power is out, everywhere," The same voice that asked the question.

"I already checked the generator, its dead. The UPS systems didn't work. My cell phone is suddenly not working." He noticed several people take their cell phones out and try to turn them on. Predictably none of them were successful. "Jason's brand-new car won't start. Jason tell them what we could see from the roof."

Jason stepped forward and raised his voice, "While we were trying to get my car to start we heard a loud explosion and could see an orange glow from the southeast. We went up to the roof and could see a large fire over near March. Can't be sure, but it looks like a plane crash to me."

Rob took back over, "If anyone has their keys on them go right now and see if your car will start." He expected exactly zero success as everyone present drove cars that were at the most five years old, the only exception being Rob himself who drove a fifteen-year-old diesel pick-up truck, but he still told them to do it. He wanted them to see for themselves, wanted to make it more real and immediate for each person. It turned out that six of the dispatchers had their car keys with them, but the entire group except for Jason and Rob went into the parking lot to check the cars. After a few minutes they all made their way back. As expected, there was no success.

"Nothing right?" Rob asked.

"Yeah but the headlights and dome lights came on. Why?" The question came from one of the newer dispatchers.

"Like I said, I don't know the science behind it. I only know what that class taught and the little bit that I picked up doing my own research. The only thing I can say with any certainty is that things are going to get way worse before they get better."

"So, what are we going to do then?" Another question from somewhere in the group.

"I don't know about anyone else, but I know what I'm going to do. I'll be going home. You guys have to decide what you are going to do on your own. I'm not going to try to order or force anyone to do anything in this situation. Any other questions?"

"If we leave, isn't that abandoning our post? We could lose our jobs over that, right?" The question came from the same person who asked the previous.

"That's true. If you leave and an hour from now the power comes back on, yes you could lose your job. But I really don't think the power is coming back on. Probably for years. But in the end, that's just my gut feeling on this, and that's why you need to make your own decision. If you attended that training class think about what was taught. If you haven't attended that class, ask someone who did. Seriously guys, in my opinion this is a worst-case scenario. I think what happened a little bit ago is going to be the most significant event to happen to humanity in a very long time. Anyone have anything else?"

When no one responded Rob continued, "Okay, since there is nothing else, I'll tell you what I'm going to do. I live in Yucaipa. I have about a twenty-five mile walk to get home to my wife and son. I'm going to change out of this uniform, gather my stuff, show whoever decides to stay where all of the emergency supplies are stored, then start walking home." He looked at his watch and was happy to see it was still working. It was an old school time piece with hands that his grandfather had given him. 12:01 am. "It's midnight. In thirty minutes I'll meet everyone back here and we'll have another quick meeting. In the mean time you all need to decide if you are staying or going." Rob got down off the chair and started walking towards the building with Jason following. He walked through the propped open door, down the hallway and into the locker room, lighting the way with the emergency flashlight.

Rob opened his locker and started changing out of his uniform into his civilian clothes in the dim light of the cheap flashlight. There was no way he was going to attempt the walk home wearing a uniform that made him look like a cop. He wanted to keep as low a profile as possible during the journey. He quickly changed into a black Carhart jacket, dark gray shirt, and jeans, putting his work shoes back on. He grabbed his car keys, wallet which contained his ID, bank cards, and eighty dollars in cash, and a picture of his wife Monica holding Jackson shortly after she gave birth. It was his favorite picture of them. He stared at the picture for a moment, hoping and praying that they would be safe, then put it into his pocket. He placed the uniform inside the locker, took one last look to make sure there was nothing he should take with him, then closed it before leaving. As he left the locker room he passed by Jason who was also changing. "I'll be at my truck," Rob said. He didn't bother to wait for a response before exiting.

As he walked out of the locker room and down the hallway he was grateful that he took that terrorism class and did his own research. Because of that he was a little more prepared than the average person was going to be. After he realized just how vulnerable modern society was due to its dependence on a fragile power grid he began preparing for a situation like this. Rob wasn't rich and did not have a lot of money saved up, but he was able to accomplish a lot by budgeting a little money every month to go towards the preparations. Each month he bought a little more of what he decided they needed and soon he had a large amount of supplies stored away. At home he stocked up on extra water and food, had certain survival and camping supplies stored in his garage and shed, and made sure his wife was at least familiar with each firearm he owned. He also made sure he stock piled enough ammunition for a situation like this, for both self-defense and hunting needs.

The hardest part of the preparations was convincing his wife that the threat was real. Monica thought Rob was a little crazy when he first talked to her about it. She thought the chances of an EMP so remote that preparing for one was a waste of money. Rob tried to convince her by explaining to her it was like insurance. You don't buy homeowners insurance because you know your house is going to burn down. You buy it in case it does burn down. Still, she balked at the idea.

What finally made her agree was a news report that had nothing to do with a solar flare or terror attack. It was a report about California's vulnerability to a very large earthquake courtesy of the many fault lines running through the state. The scientist that was interviewed said that the state was many years overdue for a massive earthquake that would result in tens of billions of dollars in damage and thousands of deaths and that people needed to be prepared. Rob could see the news report had Monica's undivided attention especially when the scientist mentioned the Crafton Hills fault zone which ran directly beneath their city. When the report was over, and the channel cut to a commercial, Rob muted the TV, turned to his wife and said, "You know, we wouldn't just be preparing for an EMP. Anything we do would be preparing for any type of disaster, including an earthquake." It was enough to convince her and that weekend they sat down and planned out exactly what supplies they would invest in, what would be bought first and what could wait, and where stuff would be stored.

Rob once again left the building through the open back door and walked to the far side of the parking lot to his truck. When he got there he dropped the tailgate before walking around the side and opening the back-passenger side door. Part of his preparations was putting together what a lot of people referred to as a "bug out bag." The idea was to have seventy-two hours' worth of supplies in a backpack in case you had to grab it and go. Rob referred to his as a "get home bag" and always had it in his backseat whenever he left home.

From the floor board of the back seat he picked up a large black Eberlestock backpack and a pair of brown Merrell hiking shoes. The pack had cost more than he wanted to spend at the time, but Rob knew they made high quality gear and decided to make sure he got a pack that would hold up under the worst conditions, rather than buy a cheaper pack and have it fall apart when he needed it most.

He took it back to the tailgate where he exchanged his work shoes for the hiking shoes then started to pull out some of the items from inside the backpack. The first thing was a black beanie which he put on. The overnight temperatures in this area could easily get down to the forties and being bald didn't exactly help keep him warm.

Next, he pulled out three extra magazines for the Springfield XD he carried, along with a box of 100 rounds of Hornady 9mm hollow point ammo. He quickly loaded sixteen rounds into each magazine before putting them aside. They were what the State of California deemed "high capacity" magazines and weren't exactly legal to possess, but at this point Rob didn't care. These three would be added to the two ten round magazines that he had whenever he carried the XD as his CCW and would give him sixty-eight readily accessible rounds, plus another in the chamber, to use if he got into a tight spot, which he planned to avoid if at all possible. The sixteen round magazines were for shit hit the fan scenarios, which, Rob decided, the current situation was categorized as. The next item he pulled out was a Kershaw Camp 10. It was basically a small machete with a ten-inch blade. He strapped the sheath to the left shoulder strap of the backpack with the handle pointing down for easy access then looked at his watch. 12:35 am. Time to head back to the patio.

As Rob walked back to the patio he noticed everyone was already present. Once again, he climbed onto the chair. "Has everyone made their decision?" No one responded so he took that as a yes and continued, "Anyone decide they are going to stay?" Fourteen of the twenty-two dispatchers raised their hands. "Okay, anyone that is going to try to make it home needs to go get ready to do so. Change out of your uniform if you have any extra clothes, get your personal belongings and anything from your car that you want to take. Remember, you have to carry whatever you take so be smart about what you choose to take and what you leave behind. If you have anything that you can easily carry to use as a weapon to defend yourself with you should probably do so."

Before Rob could continue a confused voice in the crowd interrupted him, "A weapon? Why would we need a weapon?"

"Think about it. How long has the power been out? About an hour, right? In that time, how many 9-1-1 calls have you taken?" Rob answered his own question, "Zero. That's not because no one is trying to call 9-1-1. Trust me, more people have tried calling 9-1-1 since the power went out than ever before, but they can't get through because nothing electronic works anymore. That means you can't get through either. So, as you're walking home if someone attacks you what are you going to do? You can't call 9-1-1, so your best hope is to avoid any human contact if you can and defend yourself if you need to. A weapon will help you do that." He waited a beat to let his words sink in. "Any other questions?" There were none, so Rob continued, "Those of you who are leaving get ready to go. Those of you who are staying follow me inside and I'll show you where everything is at." Rob hopped off the chair and made his way to the building, followed by Jason and the fourteen who decided to stay. He entered the building using the outside stairwell and the broken door that accessed directly into the basement. Using the flashlight, Rob made his way to the shelves that were closest to the interior stairwell doorway and located ten red plastic disaster emergency supply bins and fifteen cases of bottled water. Rob knew the bins would contain food meant to sustain the dispatchers during a prolonged disaster that kept the dispatchers in the building, such as the large earthquake that Californian's had been expecting for the last couple decades but had yet to happen.

"Everyone take a bin and when those are gone anyone still empty-handed grab a case of water. Take it up to the break room," Rob instructed. He carried a case of water as he followed the group back upstairs. Once in the breakroom he instructed everyone to put the bins on the tables in the middle of the room then he opened a few and mainly found long shelf-life dehydrated food, but also a few that held protein bars. The labels on the protein bars showed that they had a shelf life of five years and Rob knew they had been replaced about a year prior. "That's the supplies. There are also a few sleeping cots, more flashlights and batteries, that type of stuff down there. What all of you should do is find any type of container, like these plastic bins, and fill them up with water before the water supply runs out," he announced to everyone in the room. "Anyone have any other questions?"

"What do you mean when the water supply runs out?"

"The power is out," Rob said. "Once the pressure in the water pipes is gone, there will be no more running water. The water company won't be able to keep pumping more water into the water mains. And, this building is at the top of this hill, so water pressure is going to drop here before any of the surrounding neighborhoods. Any other questions?" When no one answered he turned and walked outside to the back patio where he found five of the eight dispatchers that had elected to make the hike home.

"Where is everyone else?" Rob asked.

"Getting stuff from their cars," Rachel replied.

"Let them know, and you guys too, there are some emergency supplies in the breakroom. Go get some of the protein bars and a few bottles of water and get ready to go. I'll give everyone 30 more minutes to be ready, then we leave."

Rob walked back to his truck to finish his own preparations.

From the backpack he pulled out a Safariland holster and double magazine holder, undid his belt, slid the holster onto his right side and the magazine holder onto his left side before buckling his belt back up. He walked to the driver door of the truck and sat in the driver seat. On a whim he pulled out his keys and tried to start it. Nothing. Not that he really expected it to start, but it was still a disappointment.

He reached into his center console and picked up his Springfield XD. Attached to the rails in front of the trigger guard was a TLR-1 weapon light. It allowed him access to light while holding his gun by simply moving his finger slightly, that way he could keep a two-handed grip on the gun for better accuracy. *I wish I could have gotten one of those new Gen 5 Glock 19's. This damn commie state and their handgun roster. Oh well, at least I have a gun,* he thought to himself as he holstered the gun and pulled out the miniature first aid pack that was next to the gun. In it was a face shield for CPR and a tourniquet that he would add to his larger first aid kit that was in his backpack. He also pulled out the extra ten-round magazine and placed that in his pant pocket. The last items he pulled out were a folding Gerber knife in a nylon belt holder and a pair of black Oakley sunglasses. He planned to do most of his traveling at night but the glasses could be useful.

He got out of the truck and went back around to the tailgate. He once again undid his belt, this time placing the Gerber knife on his left side just behind the magazine holder before re-buckling the belt. He drew his XD from the holster, hit the magazine release with his thumb to drop the ten-round magazine out of it, replaced it with one of the sixteen-round magazines, holstered the weapon, placed the two additional sixteen-round magazines into the magazine holder on his belt, and put the extra ten-round magazine into his pocket next to the one he obtained from the center console of the truck. He put the CPR mask and tourniquet into the first aid pack inside his backpack and the sunglasses into one of the side pouches, then pulled out a plastic canteen which had a metal holder that also doubled as a small tin pot and a refillable water pouch that had a hose bib at the top he could clip to his shoulder strap and easily drink water out of while on the go.

Rob left everything except the canteen and water pouch and walked back into the large building. He entered the break room where the fourteen dispatchers who were staying were gathered and went over to the sink to fill both the canteen and water pouch with water. After both were full he shut off the water, turned, and addressed everyone in the room. "The water pressure is already dropping, so you guys better get on top of filling those plastic bins." He took his building keys out of his pocket and handed them to the person standing closest to him, "Those keys open every door in this building, including the radio tech area on the other side. Other than that, if anybody has any questions, this is your last chance to ask, I'll be leaving in a few minutes."

At first no one said anything, then he heard, "Take care Rob, good luck getting home. I hope you're wrong about all this."

"Me too," Rob replied. "Trust me, I hope I walk out that gate then the lights turn on and I can turn around and walk right back in." He took a deep breath. "Good luck to you guys too. I think this will be the last time I ever see any of you. You guys are good dispatchers and it was a pleasure working with and supervising all of you. Take care of each other and yourselves." Rob took a moment to give everyone a hug, then turned and left the building before he got any more emotional.

As he walked through the parking lot he passed the patio and told everyone, "If anybody needs to say goodbye to anyone, go do so now. Everyone is in the break room. Then meet me at my truck in fifteen minutes." All eight including Jason walked towards the building.

When Rob arrived back at his truck he placed the water pouch into its specially designed pouch inside the Eberlestock backpack, snaked the hose through the opening in the top of the backpack and clipped the bib to the top of the right shoulder strap. The canteen he stowed next to his Kershaw Siege. The Siege was a hatchet or tomahawk that could also be used as a pry bar. Next, he went back into the cab of his truck and took out his vehicle registration and looked through the paperwork that was in the glove box. Anything he found that had any identifying information, especially his address, Rob removed. He took the paperwork over to the smoking area that had been set up for the few dispatchers who smoked and used the large ash tray to burn the papers. *There's a good chance this place will be overrun by some bad people at some point in the future. Don't need them trying to track me down trying to take out some crazy revenge on people who work in Law Enforcement,* Rob thought to himself.

Once the papers were ashes, Rob walked back to his truck while he thought about anything he was carrying that could be left behind. He had a twenty-five-mile hike, part of it through a canyon and hills, and he wanted to cut as much weight as possible. Rob took out his non-functioning cell phone, removed the microSD card that contained all the pictures that were on the phone, and tossed it into the bed of the truck. He put the card into his coin pocket of his pants. *I'll probably never be able to get the pictures from it, but it doesn't weigh anything. Maybe someday when I'm old I'll be able to get the pictures off it.*

He took out his keys, took the house key off the ring and put it into his coin pocket next to the microSD card, then tossed the rest of the keys into the bed of the truck. The last thing he left was the emergency flashlight he was still carrying around in his pocket. He had his own flashlight made by Surefire. He intentionally bought a model that was battery powered, knowing that if the power went out he wouldn't be able to charge it, and included extra batteries in his backpack. In his experience Surefire made some of the most durable and reliable flashlights one could buy. He couldn't think of anything else that could be left behind so he sat on the tailgate of the truck, leaned back against his backpack and stared at the sky while he waited for everyone that was leaving to come back out.

As Rob sat there something started bothering him but he couldn't put his finger on it. As he enjoyed the aurora it suddenly hit him. It was so quiet. Riverside was a city of almost 350,000 people and one of the main streets through this area of the city ran right in front of the dispatch center. Normally they could hear cars and trucks passing by at all times of the day and night. March Air Reserve base was close by, and even Ontario International Airport was only 15 or 20 miles away, so the sound of large jets was normal to hear. But now the only thing Rob could hear was the sound of a few crickets. It was nice, but also a little strange.

As he waited, Rob tried to think about his route home. The best thing he could think to do was walk east on Alessandro Boulevard to the I-215 freeway; walk north on the I-215 for a couple miles until it merged with State Highway 60; take Highway 60 east through Moreno Valley until he reached the eastern edge of the city and could cut through to San Timoteo Canyon; take the canyon through to Yucaipa and he would be home free. Rob believed his biggest challenge would be getting through Moreno Valley. He would enter that city when he transitioned onto Highway 60 and had to walk nine or ten miles before he came out on the other side.

The problem with Moreno Valley was that it had a high crime rate. Due to its location in southern California, its easy access to the freeways that ran through it, and lots of low income housing and projects, there was a large drug and gang problem there. Rob knew that there were a lot of hard working law-abiding citizens that lived and worked in Moreno Valley, but the gangs caused all sorts of issues. The 9-1-1 calls for shootings, stabbings, armed robberies, and other violent crimes were a daily occurrence. There was no getting around it, there were a lot of bad people in that city that would not hesitate to target Rob for no other reason other than they wanted the supplies he carried in his backpack. The good news was the time that the EMP occurred. Due to being so late at night, and a Monday night, there would not have been much traffic out. Walking through the city at night, Rob could pretty much bet that anyone out and about would probably be part of the criminal element that plagued Moreno Valley. And using the freeway as much as possible he hoped to stay out of any trouble.

Rob wasn't sure how much time passed, but it couldn't have been long, when he heard a group of people approaching. He waited for the eight dispatchers that were hiking home to arrive at the back of the truck before he sat up. "Okay, first before we leave, which direction does everyone live? I live in Yucaipa, so I'm headed east. Jason you still live on the other side of Riverside?"

"Yeah, over near Arlington and Tyler," Jason replied.

The next person to speak was Ashley Thompson, a twenty-year-old white girl who loved the outdoors, "I live in Woodcrest, just a few miles from here."

"Okay you're headed south then, anyone else live that direction?" Rob asked the group.

Only one person did. Heather Barnes, an older lady who everyone seen as the dispatch mom and was a few years short of retiring. Four of the remaining six lived closer to the middle of Riverside. The fifth was Jeremy Huff, a thirty-two-year-old white man who lived in Lake Elsinore.

"Geez," Rob responded. "You got a long ways to go. You know which way you're going to head?"

"I'm thinking heading south with Ashley and Heather then

after they get home going through the Lake Matthews area. Maybe try to cut through the hills from there. Otherwise I have to go all the way around and maybe through Canyon Lake, that's way outta my way. I just hope I don't get lost in the hills."

"Yeah that plan sounds as good as any," this came from Jason. "At least all those areas for the most part are a little more rural, so you won't have to worry about people as much. Not like us that have to go through Riverside. Just remember sun rises in the east sets in the west. It can help you stay on a southerly course."

"That just leaves Rachel. Where do you live?" Rob asked.

"Moreno valley, on the south end of the city," She replied.

"Okay I guess we are walking together then. I have to head through Moreno Valley to get to San Timoteo Canyon anyways." He then addressed the whole group, "Listen close everyone. Keep an eye out, watch your back, watch your friends back, don't hesitate to run or fight. Soon people are going to realize that because there are no working cars, that also means there are no working cop cars. They'll realize the police aren't going to be coming to any calls for help, even if they could be called. People are going to start going crazy. Looting, raping, killing, you name it, it's going to happen. If you have a weapon you need to carry it, if you don't you need to find one. Even something as simple as a tire iron is better than nothing. And don't hesitate to use it if you need to. Remember, other than those you can trust, you are on your own once you leave this center. Good luck to all of you, I hope you all make it home safe and find your families waiting for you."

"You remember where I live?" Rob addressed Jason directly. A couple months prior Rob had a small get together at his house to celebrate Jason's promotion to supervisor and before that Jason had visited several times to watch sports and hang out with Rob.

"Yeah I remember."

"Well, if for some reason you find that you can't stay at your place and need to leave, you are more than welcome to head to Yucaipa." Rob shook his hand. "Godspeed buddy, I hope we survive this."

"Me too," Jason replied. "Thanks for the offer, I might have to take you up on that. Good luck you uncivilized swine," he said with a smile. "Stay safe and make it home to your family."

With that, Jason turned and started walking through the parking lot followed by the dispatchers that were headed east and south. As they left Rob gave each one a hug and wished them good luck. He was happy to see several of them make a last stop at their cars to get anything they could use as a weapon before running to catch up with Jason. He could see several carrying tire irons, one carrying a bat, and even one carrying what looked like a two-foot long metal pole.

Rob turned to Rachel, "You grabbed some water and protein bars, right?"

She held up a purple over the shoulder messenger bag with flowers on it, "Got them in here."

Rob was pleased to see she had changed into jeans and running shoes. She was also wearing a green sweater that unfortunately had the logo of the agency on the front. *Oh well, nothing we can do about that right now. I don't have one to give her that doesn't have it,* Rob thought. "You have any weapons?"

"Yes," she relied somewhat sheepishly. She pulled an ASP, a collapsible baton, from the bag.

"Where the hell did you get that?" Rob asked her.

"It was in one of the open lockers inside. I think one of the investigators that use our locker room accidently left it open.

I figured she couldn't use it right now, so I took it." Explained Rachel.

"Good thinking," Rob said with a smile. "Just keep it handy in case you need it. You know how it works?" When Rachel shook her head no he held out his hand, "Let me have it and I'll show you the basics." He took a few minutes and showed her how to expand the ASP by swinging her arm and flicking her wrist, and how to collapse it down by tapping it on the ground. "If you have to use it you don't need to have it expanded when you first swing it. It should expand no problem when you go to hit someone. You can also use it to break windows if you need." Rob let her expand and collapse it several times to get a feel for the impact weapon. Rachel was half Mexican and half Panamanian, short at about five foot two Rob would guess, but he wasn't going to ask, and in good shape. She would have no problem walking the distance to her house. "Last thing. Did you get a flashlight from inside?"

"No," Rachel said while shaking her head. "I didn't think of that. I can run back in real quick."

"Here take this one," Rob replied as he picked up and handed her the one he was going to leave behind.

Rob looked at his watch. 1:15 am. Time to go. He shouldered his backpack and walked through the parking lot with Rachel following him. They went around to the front of the building, into the front parking lot, and through the pedestrian gate. He held it open long enough for Rachel to pass through, made sure the gate closed and latched behind them, then they walked down the long sloping driveway to Alessandro, the main street that ran in front of the communications center. At the end of the driveway Rob paused, took one last look at the large cinder block building he called his home away from home for the past 8 years, then turned and started walking east.

CHAPTER 3

Alessandro Boulevard was a wide street with three lanes running both directions and a large well landscaped center median. Rob and Rachel walked near the right curb line through the semi darkness. The sky was still alight with the aurora and it was as bright as if there was a full moon out. Rob was grateful as it made being able to see hazards much easier. The downside was that others could spot Rob and Rachel easier as well. As the street made a long sweeping left hand turn that put it on a true east west line Rob noticed Rachel was staring at the sky. "You ever see anything like it?" he asked.

"When I was a teenager my family went on a summer cruise to Alaska. One of those ones that go to the glaciers and what not. On the very last night before we got to our last port we saw the aurora. But it definitely wasn't as bright as it is now. I thought it was amazing back then, but tonight makes that look mediocre in comparison." Rob could hear the wonder in her voice.

They continued to walk in silence, passing Trautwein Road and entering a mixture of commercial and residential area. On the south side of the street was a large shopping center that stretched several blocks along Alessandro. In the shopping center there was a movie theater, several fast food places, restaurants, and grocery stores. There were only a few cars in the parking lot that Rob could see, and he figured they belonged to the few employees tasked with overnight stocking of shelves or cleaning of the businesses. Employees who, like Rob and Rachel, were at work going about their normal everyday lives when everything changed drastically in the blink of an eye. Rob wondered if any of the employees had any clue of what was really going on or thought it was just another power outage.

The first people they encountered were at a Shell Gas station they reached when they were about halfway past the shopping center. The gas station had a line of six pumps, making for a total of twelve positions where one could refuel their vehicle, a propane refill station with a large tank, a water and air station, and a large convenience store with glass windows that covered the front. There were two men standing on the sidewalk staring at the sky. One was white and, Rob guessed, about six feet four and around 300 pounds. *He's a big boy,* Rob thought. The other was an average sized black man wearing the black with red and yellow trim uniform of a Shell Gas station employee. Rob recognized him immediately. Because dispatch was a twenty-four-hour operation the dispatchers tended to get to know the few people who worked night shifts at the handful of nearby twenty-four-hour businesses.

"Hey Carl, what's up dude?" Rob asked.

"Nothing much Rob. Hi Rachel. Just trying to figure out what's causing this light. It's crazy!" Carl's voice was a mixture of excitement and bewilderment.

"Hi Carl," Rachel said with a quick wave.

"Yeah, I've never seen anything like it. You lost all power inside too?" even though it was obvious, Rob was leading up to his next question.

"Yeah man, even the little generator we're supposed to use to run the pumps when the power goes out so we can still sell gas won't start."

"Gotcha. You try your car yet?" Rob knew Carl drove an early eighties Toyota four door and was curious if it still ran.

"It died when I was pulling into that spot around back. I was supposed to start at midnight but class let out early and I got here early." From previous conversations Rob knew Carl was taking night classes at one of the local colleges, studying to be a hydro-engineer. "I was parking when my car died, and I watched the power go out at the same time. Its strange man. I can understand the power outage and my old bucket of a car breaking down, but both at the same exact time, plus these lights in the sky? Feels like the end of the world almost."

"Yeah I hear you, it just might be. Alright man, we're gonna get going again, we have a long way to walk. You take care of yourself Carl," Rob gave a nod to the large white guy who had yet to say anything as he started to turn away. Rob received a respectful nod in return.

"You guys too," Carl said.

"Bye guys," Rachel said quietly before following Rob.

With a sigh, Rob continued walking with Rachel next to him. He hoped Carl was going to be okay. He was a nice guy who was always polite and friendly anytime Rob or any other dispatcher stopped into the gas station for snacks or anything else that helped them get through their long shifts. As they continued down Alessandro Rob moved from the sidewalk into the street and moved closer to the center island with Rachel close by. He could see the puzzled look on her face, so he explained. "Once we pass the shopping center there's that big apartment complex on the right side; on the left is that huge property that belongs to the water district. That property has a large fence with razor wire on top. Chances are anyone we come across is going to be on the right side closer to the apartments, and as much as possible I want to avoid contact. The less contact we have with people, the lower the chances of getting into an altercation with someone."

"Okay, that makes sense. Let's hope it works and nothing crazy happens," Rachel said.

They soon left the shopping center behind and now on the left was a water treatment plant situated on a large piece of property closed off with a ten-foot rod iron fence topped with razor wire. On the right was a large three-story apartment complex with an eight-foot rod iron fence surrounding the buildings and gates blocking access to the driveways. Rob could see a dark colored sedan stopped on the eastbound side of the road in the middle lane. When they were within two hundred feet of the car he said in a low voice, "Let's cross to the other side of the street." Rachel followed him across the foliage and into the westbound lanes. Due to nature's lightshow in the sky, it was bright enough that as they came even with the car he could see someone sitting in the driver seat staring at him and Rachel. He also noticed several of the balconies in the apartment complex were occupied, presumably by residents who were awakened by the bright aurora or the explosion created by the plane. Or both.

As they walked Rob kept scanning, turning his head slowly left and right looking for potential threats, and every few minutes turning around and walking backward for a few feet while he took a good look to make sure they weren't being followed. He especially watched the person in the car and the people on the balconies, making sure no one was going to try to do anything that would threaten Rachel and himself. Rachel realized what Rob was doing and was soon looking around as much as possible. "Let me know right away if you see something," he told her.

"Like what?" she asked.

"Anything that looks out of place, especially people, but even dogs and stopped cars. If you aren't sure about what you see tell me. Better safe than sorry." Rachel nodded her understanding. At Barton Street the water treatment property on the left and the apartment complex on the right ended and new properties began as they crossed the intersection. Now on the left was a storage facility, and behind that was Sycamore Canyon Wilderness Park. It was a huge wilderness area covering almost 1,500 acres and had numerous hiking trails running through it. On the right was a small strip mall with a liquor store and several mom and pop shops with a residential neighborhood behind the businesses. The strip mall was dark, of course, but Rob also did not see any candle light or flashlights being used. As far as he could remember none of the stores were twenty-four hours and most likely closed.

As they made progress along Alessandro Rob was thinking about what was ahead and what types of issues they might run into. "Rachel, this wilderness park isn't fenced off or secured in any way and there's a large transient camp just off the road. Because the way the land drops down just off the roadway, and all the trees and brush, most people don't know it's there, but there are a few dozen transients that live down there. Keep your eyes and ears open. If you see or hear anything out of the ordinary let me know right away." Once again Rachel nodded but didn't say anything.

About a half mile after they crossed Barton Rachel got Rob's attention and pointed to their left into the wildlife preserve, "Hey check it out."

Rob had been walking backwards checking what was behind them. He quickly turned and could see what she was pointing at. A glow through the trees. Soon they could also hear voices, but due to all the trees and bushes blocking their view, they couldn't get a good enough view. "Looks like a camp fire with five or six people, and they sound very drunk. At least someone is having a good time," Rob said while chuckling. They could hear a couple people singing and several others laughing and cheering them on.

"They for sure are, maybe they will let us join them for

karaoke night," Rachel joked, also laughing.

"Hopefully they don't catch their camp on fire; there is no one coming to help them if they do," Rob added.

They fell quiet once again as they walked, both pondering what life was going to be like, not just over the next few days, but the next few months and years. It was only a few hours since the power first went out, but in some ways if felt like a lifetime. In just that short time their lives had changed dramatically, and both were sure they would change even more before everything was said and done. In the blink of an eye they both went from dispatchers answering phone calls and working radio channels to survivors who were just trying to make it home to their families. Before, they were the ones answering 9-1-1 calls and sending people help. Now, they couldn't contact help for themselves even if their lives depended on it. It was a sobering and terrifying thought, but Rob used that fear to focus his attention on accomplishing his mission of getting home to his family.

They soon arrived at the end of the wildlife preserve. Now, on the left, they could see a large commercial area, including several large warehouses set back off the road, along with a drive through burger joint and an office building. Just past the office building was a Chevron Gas station. On the right side of the road, just past the curb line, the land sloped up sharply for about ten feet before leveling off. Due to the terrain they couldn't see what was on the other side, but Rob believed it was just open land. He knew they were getting close to the I-215 so he decided they should take a break before making the push into Moreno Valley. "Let's head over towards that office building on the left and find somewhere we can rest for a few minutes."

They walked onto the sidewalk on the north side of the street and used the driveway entrance to access the office building property. They cut across the parking lot and moved around to the backside of the newer two-story office building where they found a concrete picnic table in a small grass area. After putting their bags down on the table Rob told Rachel, "I need to go to the restroom, give me a minute." He walked to the side of the building and found a bush to relieve himself behind. When he returned he could tell Rachel wanted to say something but was staying quiet. "What's up?" he prompted her.

"I need to go too..." she paused "...do you have anything I can use?" Even in the semi-darkness he could see Rachel blushing.

It dawned on him what she needed. "I have a roll of toilet paper in my bag, but hold on, I have a better idea. Wait here a second." He walked over to the burger joint where he found a few outdoor tables that still had the condiments and napkin holders on them. He pulled a stack of napkins a several inches thick from one of the holders and walked back to Rachel. "Here you go," he said as he handed her the stack. "Keep what you don't use in your bag for later."

"Thank you," she said, still a little embarrassed.

While Rachel found somewhere to relieve herself Rob sat down at the table and opened one of the protein bars he took from the dispatch center. He was about halfway through it when Rachel returned. "Thanks, I don't feel like I'm going to burst anymore," Rachel said.

"You're welcome. Let's take about thirty minutes to rest here. Eat a little bit and drink all your water. We gotta stay hydrated as much as possible and before we start walking again we're going to stop by that Chevron next door to get some more water and food. Where in Moreno Valley do you live?"

"Over near the golf course off Moreno Beach and Cactus."

That got Rob thinking. This was the first time he really thought about where in the city she lived and what route she would need to take to get there. The golf course was at the south end of the city against some hills and situated in the middle of several newer neighborhoods, the kind where the backyards of a lot of the houses butted up against the course. The route that Rob planned to take was the freeway which ran east and west a little north of the middle of the city. Not only was this the most direct route home, but at the time of night that everything stopped working there would be little traffic on the freeways, so he had less of a chance of encountering other people.

As they rested he turned it over and over in his mind. Walking Rachel all the way home would add miles and time to his own journey, but he couldn't just let her walk alone through one of the worst parts of town in the middle of the night with no hope of an emergency response if something happened. He battled with it for several minutes. His responsibility to his own family to get home as soon as possible, or risk Rachel making the attempt to get the rest of the way home on her own? In the end he knew it would eat him up inside if he didn't know Rachel made it home safe. Even though it would add who knew how much time to his own trip home, he decided to take Rachel at least to the entrance to her neighborhood.

"Well, I planned to take the freeway through to the east side of Moreno Valley, but I want to make sure you get home safe, so I'll detour and walk with you to your neighborhood," Rob told Rachel.

"Are you sure Rob?" she asked. Her voice was hopeful but she didn't want him to feel pressured into changing his initial plan. "I'm sure walking all the way to my house is going to add on a lot of time to your trip, especially since you need to go through San Tim on the north side of the city. I live on the south side, and you need to get home to your wife and son."

"Yeah I'm sure. It won't add on that much time," Rob replied, downplaying the amount of time it would add to his journey. "Besides, there's safety in numbers, and if we make it to your neighborhood you'll be home and I'll be almost through the city. I'll just need to cut over to Redlands Blvd and then head north and I'll be out of the city before I know it."

"Wow, thank you. I was really worried about trying to make it through the city on my own," she said, obviously relieved.

With that decision made, he needed to plan out the best route to take. While it was impossible to completely avoid residential areas the entire way there, he still wanted to do so as much as possible. Because the EMP occurred in the middle of the night most commercial areas should be devoid of people, except for overnight security at some buildings and the few businesses that had employees working overnight shifts. Because of this he decided that prior to reaching the freeway they would cut down Meridian Parkway and head south through the commercial warehouses to Cactus Avenue, then turn east. From there it was a straight shot, much of it being in commercial areas, until they reached Rachel's neighborhood. The only residential area would be a two mile stretch that would be heavily populated.

The other part of this route that worried Rob was the County Hospital. If they took Cactus they would walk right by the front of it. Being the County Hospital, they had a small jail ward inside that treated inmates from the county jails and a psychiatric facility to treat anyone with mental health issues. Due to the power loss, who knew what the status of the hospital and patients would be. Rob decided to just get past the residential area first, then worry about the hospital when the time came.

Rob checked the time. 2:45 am. It had taken them about an hour to walk to where they were currently taking their break, plus the thirty minutes to rest. It was time to get moving again, but before they did, he wanted to go over something with Rachel.

"Hey Rachel. We are going to get moving, but first, like I mentioned, we're going to go over to the Chevron and get some stuff.

I'm pretty sure it's closed but I can't remember offhand if they are twenty-four hours. If they are closed, I'm going to break in. If they are open and someone is inside, we'll get what we need and offer to pay. I have eighty dollars in my wallet, but if they refuse we are just going to walk out. If they try to stop us I'm going to show them my gun and hopefully they'll just decide it's not worth trying to stop us. Before we go, I need to make sure you're going to be okay with that. Breaking in is a felony. Armed robbery is a felony. But right now, none of that matters. There are no cops responding to the 9-1-1 call. No detectives coming to take over the investigation. No one coming to arrest us. The only thing that matters is getting home, you to your husband and kid, and me to my wife and son." Rob fell silent while he watched Rachel think about what he just said.

After a minute or so she responded, "I don't really like it, but we have to do what we have to do. I took that terrorism class too, I just never thought something like this would actually happen. I have to get home to my family, and I'll do whatever it takes to make that happen." By the time she finished talking there was determination in her voice.

"Good enough for me," Rob replied. "Let's get going." They stood up, picked up their bags, walked around the side of building, and back towards the street.

As they walked Rob talked, "Before we get there drink whatever water you have left." He had emptied his water pouch on the walk from the dispatch center so he took out his canteen and drank heavily from it. "Drink it all if possible. We'll get all we need from the gas station. For food, get stuff like trail mix and more protein bars, stuff that's high in fiber and protein. Try to stay away from junk food, sweets, chips, all that stuff. Get as much as you can comfortably carry." They could now see the parking lot and the pumps of the station. The station property was situated on the northwest corner of Alessandro Blvd and Sycamore Canyon Blvd and had two rows of pumps in the lot in addition to the usual propane tank and air and water station. Rob decided to walk to the street corner so that they could get a look of the east side of the building where the employees normally parked. They found no cars anywhere in the parking lot.

"Okay, looks like we're breaking in." Before approaching the building, Rob took out the Kershaw Siege hatchet. "We'll go in through the front door. You keep an eye on our backs and if you see anything call it out right away. And get your ASP out and keep it handy, never know if you'll need it."

Rob gave her a second to get ready then walked up to the building. He started from the side and took a good look through the large front windows. Just because there were no cars in the lot didn't mean there wasn't an employee, or someone else that had Rob's same idea, inside. When he was satisfied he approached the front door and went to work. He checked to make sure the door was locked before breaking the glass, then one swing is all it took to shatter it. He took a moment to make sure all the glass was removed, the last thing they needed was a large piece of glass falling on their head as they walked through, then ducked under the metal handle that was placed horizontally across the width of the door about halfway up. When he entered he dropped his Eberlestock backpack and hatchet on the front checkout counter and using his flashlight took a quick look behind the counter and down each aisle.

After clearing the front store area, he went through the open door at the rear of the business that had an "Employee's Only" sign attached to the front of it. "Wait here and keep an eye out front, if anyone comes give me a holler," he said to Rachel. He quickly cleared the storage and break areas, then tried the office door. Locked. And no windows to see inside. He knocked to see if he would get any response. Nothing. He took a moment to stack a few boxes in front of the door then took a six pack of sodas and put them on top. His hope was that if anyone did come out of the office they would knock over the boxes when they swung open the door and cause the soda cans to fall onto the tile floor, making plenty of noise and giving him and Rachel a few precious seconds to prepare for a possible confrontation.

He made his way back to Rachel and gave her a quick rundown on the early warning system he set up at the office door. "If you hear anything from back there get over to me quick, stand behind me and watch my back."

"Okay, I got it," she said, eyes wide but voice determined.

"Let's get to work then, we leave in five minutes." Rob first went to the large refrigerators with the swinging glass doors and took out several large bottles of water. He took them to his backpack and used them to fill his water pouch and canteen, then placed a full water bottle into the backpack. It would be extra weight to carry but would be worth it. He had one bottle left over which he opened and started to drink. He downed about a third of it and walked over to the food aisle where he picked up five bags of mixed nuts and a box that held twelve protein bars of assorted flavors. He was back at his backpack putting everything inside, including the hatchet, when Rachel walked up. "Ready to go?" he asked.

"Ready when you are," Rachel replied between large gulps of water from a water bottle.

"Last thing, how long have you been up?" Rob knew working twelve-hour graveyard shifts sometimes caused them to go long stretches without sleep, especially those with children and working spouses. Rob himself had been up for about eighteen hours and at this time of night would normally be arriving home from work, unless he held over for overtime of course. He wasn't tired yet but knew it was only a matter of time, especially with the stress of trying to stay hyper alert and worrying about his family.

"What time is it? Like three or something right?" Rachel

asked. Rob looked at his watch, 3:02 am, and nodded. "I woke up about eight when my husband left for work, after getting about five hours. I worked the night before and got home just before three."

"Okay, so you are coming up on twenty hours then, after only five hours the night before." Rob walked over to a center display that held dozens of BANG energy drinks made by a company called VPX Sports. Rob loved them as they didn't leave him jittery and he didn't have the "crashing" feeling he did with other energy drinks. "Take one or two of these with you. I think we can make it to your house without stopping anywhere to sleep but we're going to be pretty tired towards the end of the walk." Rob selected two for himself and stowed them in his backpack. Again he was adding weight, but besides the obvious benefit of an energy drink, the cans had several uses once they were empty.

He started to pick up the pack when a stand on the side of the checkout counter caught his eye. 5-Hour energy shots. He decided they were light enough he could carry a few without really affecting weight but would give him a good boost of energy if he needed it on the long walk home. He took four and put them in one of the smaller zippered pouches on his pack, picked it up and turned to Rachel, "Let's head out the back and use the emergency exit. I doubt anyone is out front, but just in case someone saw us break in and is out there waiting to ambush us when we come out it'll be safer this way. Follow me close." They walked through the storage room, passing the office, and to the side emergency door that doubled as a delivery door for the large deliveries of goods that arrived every few days.

One of the perks of working for the agency was that during certain training classes they sometimes got to do things like watch the department SWAT team train, shoot all the cool weapons that SWAT deployed on their callouts and missions, and play with the driving and "shoot don't shoot" simulators.

One of the things he remembered from observing the SWAT training was the importance of not standing in doorways. They even had a term for the area around the door called the "fatal funnel". They taught that a doorway was one of the most dangerous areas to be due to the limited options for retreat, no cover and the small area that a suspect had to point his gun at without really aiming. Before opening the door, Rob put his ear up to it and listened for a few seconds. He was checking to see if he could hear anyone talking or moving around on the other side.

Once he was satisfied he slowly opened the door while standing to the side and took a good long look. Then he stepped through and immediately started moving east away from the building and through the parking lot, with Rachel right behind him, towards Sycamore Canyon Blvd, scanning their surroundings the whole way.

When they reached the street they crossed to the other side and walked to the corner. When Sycamore Canyon Boulevard crossed Alessandro, it changed names to Meridian Parkway. Rob paused for a moment to take a good look in all four directions. Not seeing any movement or anything that gave him pause they crossed the intersection and continued south on Meridian. The street was very wide with two lanes in each direction and an oversized middle turn lane. It was built this way to accommodate all the hundreds of big rigs that drove through the area to and from the warehouses on a daily basis. As they walked, this time using the sidewalk on the left side of the street, Rob once again reflected on how quiet it was. After growing up in busy southern California, with the large population and congested freeways, manmade noise was just part of the background. Hearing only the sounds of nature, which were somewhat limited due to being in a city, reminded Rob of the camping trips his family took when he was growing up. They were some of his favorite memories and he planned to start taking his son camping once he was old enough.

They passed a Metrolink train station on the left and more warehouses and commercial buildings on the right. They were about halfway between Alessandro and Cactus, now with commercial buildings on both sides, and Rob was walking backwards for a few yards checking their rear when Rachel grabbed Rob's arm and suddenly stopped walking. He spun around and looked in the direction she was pointing.

It took him a moment to see it but once he did he realized she was pointing at a very large dark colored dog. The dog was on the right side of the street, so Rob said, "Just keep walking, stay on this sidewalk. Get out your ASP and get ready. Don't be afraid to hit the dog if you need to, you definitely don't want to get bit. Keep me between yourself and the dog." As they got closer Rob could see the dog was obviously a stray with very dirty matted fur and no collar. As they got even with the dog he could see it was huge, at least 100 pounds, maybe closer to 120. The dog was staring at them but didn't move. *C'mon doggo, don't do anything dumb,* Rob thought to himself. While he wouldn't hesitate, he didn't want to shoot the dog. Not only did he not want to use the ammo and make noise that might draw unwanted attention to them, he was also a dog lover.

They were 200 feet past the dog, with Rob walking backwards keeping an eye on it, when the dog started following. *Dang, I thought we were good to go.* Rob drew his gun but kept walking backwards. "The dog is following us. Just keep walking, make sure you keep a real good lookout in front of us and let me know if you see anything," Rob told Rachel. He took a quick look to the south and could see a car stopped in the middle of the street. "Actually Rachel, turn around and watch the dog but stay close to me. Tell me right away if he charges us. I'm gonna check out that car. If it's empty, we're getting inside." He didn't wait for her to reply, quickly approached the car, which turned out to be a silver Kia Optima, and confirmed it was empty. He tried the driver door. Locked. *Damn, can't catch a break,* he thought as his mind raced. "Rachel, up on top, hurry." Rob made sure Rachel was getting onto the car with no problems as he took off his Eberlestock backpack and slung it onto the roof. Then he scrambled up himself right before the dog reached the car and started to growl manically.

Rob could now see that the dog looked like it was starving. While still a huge dog, he figured most of the dog's bulk came from the fur. The dog was now standing on its hind legs with its front paws on the trunk of the car growling and barking. Rob holstered his gun, "Hey Rachel, let me borrow your ASP." She handed it over without comment and watched as Rob slid down the windshield. The dog decided Rob was the easier target and ran over to the front of the car where it started trying to get to Rob. He took a good swing with the ASP and hit the dog in the shoulder. It immediately started whimpering and took off running north.

"That was close, my heart is racing," Rachel said, breathing hard and fast.

"Mine too. Take deep slow breaths so you don't hyperventilate." Rachel realized how fast she was breathing, closed her eyes, and started taking slower deeper breaths. "Let's wait a few minutes and see if it comes back. Hopefully I didn't really hurt it and just scared it enough to not try again."

"Okay. I'm glad this car is here. I wonder if the owner decided to walk home like we are doing."

"Maybe," Rob replied. "Just remember, this likely won't be the worst situation we encounter. If the time comes to defend yourself, don't hesitate and do whatever it takes to survive." Rachel didn't respond, but Rob could see she was thinking about what he said.

They ended up waiting for five minutes before deciding it was safe to continue. After climbing down from the car and putting their bags back on, they walked the couple hundred feet to Cactus where they turned east. When they made the turn they both could see heavy smoke up ahead in the light provided by dancing lights in the sky. A few minutes later they reached the I-215 freeway and Rob used the overpass as a vantage point to look down the freeway in both directions. A few cars here and there, but otherwise nothing that caused him concern. It wasn't until they reached the east side of the freeway and were even with the on and offramps that they could see what the smoke was coming from. A plane crash in the open field that was just south of Cactus and just north of the large runway at March Air Reserve base. *That's gotta be what we could see from the roof of dispatch,* Rob thought. He took a few minutes to study the crash but could not see any movement. *I wonder where the response is from March Fire. I know they won't be able to drive their equipment, but you would think they would walk out here to check it. Or maybe they did and just left it to burn when they realized there was nothing they could do.*

Before starting to walk again Rob studied the smoke and could see that it was drifting north across Cactus, right in their path. He could see that the smoke started to thin out, but only after it was a few hundred feet north of the street. From his backpack he took out a Hoorag that had an American Flag printed on it and put it on. It was basically a combination scarf and bandana that was worn around the neck and could easily be pulled up around the face to act as a face shield. As he put it on he asked Rachel, "You have a scarf or something like that?" Rachel shook her head no so Rob dug back into his pack and pulled out a dark blue bandana. "Tie this around your face. We'll try to avoid the smoke by swinging a little north around those businesses but just in case we end up breathing some in keep this on to help filter it some."

They walked north through the dirt area next to the freeway

then across the onramp to the northbound I-215 and into a large open field. They continued in a northeasterly direction until they reached another street, the Old 215 Frontage Road. When they reached the road, they started to smell the unique burning odor created by the crashed plane. It was an acrid combination of burning plastic, oil, and jet fuel and confirmed Rob's decision to avoid the smoke as much as possible. They walked north then turned right onto Day Street. This new street made an immediate left turn and ran north from where they were at. Just north of the intersection on the right was a large distribution warehouse.

They walked north until they got to the second driveway for the warehouse which was usually utilized by the big rigs that picked up and dropped trailers. The first thing Rob noticed was the rod iron electrical powered gate was wide open. The second thing was the security guard wearing a white uniform shirt and black uniform pants standing in the middle of the driveway just before where the gate. "Let's go over there and talk to this guy. I'm going to try to see if he'll let us walk through his parking lot. It looks like the smoke is being blocked by the building and being able to cut through would save us a lot of time."

As Rob and Rachel approached the security guard Rob pulled the Hoorag off his face and down around his neck. "Hey man, how's it going?" Rob said by way of greeting.

"Pretty good, what can I do for you?" the guard responded sleepily. Rob could now see his name tag. Martinez. He was an average height Hispanic guy in his mid-twenties and significantly overweight. If Rob had to guess, he would put him around 250 pounds.

"Did you see that plane come down?"

"Nah, I didn't see it, but I heard it. I was over at the other end of the lot doing my rounds when everything went black. At first, I figured just a power outage and I took my phone out to let my company know. I was trying to get my phone to work when I heard it crash. About made me piss my pants. I came over to the street where I could see it. Never seen anyone around it."

"Damn, that's crazy. Hey question for you, we're trying to walk home but wanted to avoid the smoke coming from that crash. We need to get down Cactus. You think you could let us cut through your lot here? We'll be in and out, no stopping. You can even walk with us if you want."

The guard paused for a second to yawn before responding, "I don't know man, I'm not supposed to let anyone on the property, especially with the power outage. The other gate is locked anyways so you couldn't get through. That's why I'm over here, it's the only open gate on the property."

"I hear you, bro," Rob said. "Promise, we won't do anything except walk through. No stopping, no touching anything. And we'll get over the wall on the other side no problem."

"Dang... Okay man, you two seem cool. Just don't stop. I see you guys stop and I'm running over to pepper spray you, got it?" the guard said, trying to put some authority into his voice.

"Yeah, no problem, no stopping at all. We'll be gone before you know it," Rob said, then thought to himself, *this guy isn't running very far, but whatever, as long as he lets us walk through.* "Thanks man, we really appreciate it," still being courteous. He didn't want the guard to change his mind last second because Rob said something smart.

"Thank you," Rachel added.

"No worries, just keep moving. I'll see you guys around," the security guard said.

No, you won't, Rob thought as he started walking with Rachel through the parking lot. They walked through the lot lined with trailers and big rigs on both sides. When they reached the end, they turned to the right and were at the closed gate that led to a driveway that in turn led out to a side street called Goldencrest Dr. Next to the wall Rob spotted a utility box of some sort that stood about four feet high and about a foot from the wall. He figured it might help them get over the eight-foot barrier standing in their way, so he walked over and checked it. It seemed sturdy enough.

"Okay Rachel," he said. "This is what we are going to do. First, we'll throw our bags over the gate, it's lower than the wall so we don't need to throw as high, then I'll help you get onto this box. From there you get on top of the wall, I'll stand in between the wall and the box and help you. Once you are up stay on top and I'll make my way up with your help. Sound good?"

"Yeah okay. I'm not strong enough to lift you though."

"You won't need to lift me, if I need it just give me a hand making it onto the wall."

"Let's do it then," she agreed.

They threw their bags over the gate then Rob helped Rachel onto the box and positioned himself between the box and the wall. "Think we can do it?" he asked.

"Yeah I can actually see over the wall and it's not as big a gap as I thought between the wall and the box." She leaned over and placed her hands on top of the wall, then pushed up with Rob using his hands to push up on her shoes. She swung her leg up and over the top so that she was straddling it. Rob's turn. He got on top of the box and mimicked Rachels movements. Once he was on top he took a moment to figure out their next move. In the still bright light of the aurora he could see some bushes on the other side, but right beneath where he was sitting was a gap in the bushes that created small open area right next to the wall.

"I'm going to lower myself down as far as I can, then drop the rest of the way. When I'm down scoot over to where I am now, then lower yourself. I'll help you the rest of the way." Once Rachel gave Rob a nod to indicate she understood the plan, he turned and put his leg over, lowered himself so he was fully stretched out and only holding on with his hands, then let go. When he hit the ground, his knees bent and hit the wall. *That frickin hurt.* "Your turn," he said to Rachel after taking a moment to recover.

Rachel moved over then lowered herself down. Instead of letting her drop, Rob grabbed her hips and helped lower her to the ground, careful to keep her in a standing position so she wouldn't also hurt her knees. "Thanks," she said.

"You got it," Rob replied. "Let's get our bags and keep moving. Once we are out of this smoke smell we need to find some place to take a quick rest. I gotta check my knees. I banged 'em pretty good." Once they were at the street they turned left and headed east on Goldencrest Drive. They reached Elsworth Street, and after crossing the intersection the smell dissipated to almost nothing. They still caught whiffs of it, but it was not as strong as before. On the right was another commercial building. The back side of the building faced Goldencrest so they circled around to the front and found a restaurant with tables and chairs outside.

Rob sat down and checked his knees while Rachel acted as a lookout. He rolled up his pant legs and used his flashlight to inspect his injury. Both knees were red and starting to swell on top of the knee caps, but no cuts or road rash. Rob dug his first aid kit out and took out some ibuprofen. "Let's take fifteen while we are here and rest. Hopefully this pain killer will kick in by then." Rob had chosen ibuprofen for his get home bag not just for the pain killer aspect, but also because it was also an anti-inflammatory.

They took their break in silence, eating some of the food they had taken from the gas station. By the time the fifteen minutes were up Rob had finished a bag of mixed nuts and used the water bottle from his bag to replace the liter he had drank from his water pouch while walking, then drank the rest of the water and put the bottle back into his bag to save for later.

Rob was happy to see their little detour did in fact get them around the worst of the smoke and put his Hoorag and bandana back into his backpack. "Let's get moving again. It's 4:30, we have about two and a half hours before the sun comes up," Rob said as he stood up and put his backpack on.

"Your knees okay?" Rachel asked him.

"Yeah, I'll be fine. Not as bad as they could be, just a little swollen. The ibuprofen should help out." They walked south through the parking lot and turned east when they reached the street. They were once again traveling on Cactus Avenue. Rob took a minute to study the street in both directions until he was satisfied there was no movement he could see in either direction, then they started walking. As they approached Frederick Street Rob could see an ambulance stopped on the south side of the street several feet away from the curb.

"Hey, let's check it out," he said to Rachel. "If no one is inside maybe we can find something useful." Rob didn't say that he would be looking for narcotics, specifically Morphine or Dilaudid. They could be very useful if either of them were to be seriously injured. *Too bad ambulances don't usually carry anti-biotics.* They first checked through the rear windows of the ambulance and found no one. They walked around the passenger side and found both front seats occupied. Both occupants were wearing uniforms that matched the logo on the side of the ambulance, so Rob figured they were the EMT and paramedic assigned to this rig when the EMP hit.

Both appeared to be sleeping so Rob knocked softly on the passenger window, trying his best to wake them up without startling them. The passenger woke up first and almost panicked when she noticed Rob and Rachel looking at her through the window. After a few seconds she slapped her partner across the chest to wake him up, then opened the door to the ambulance and stepped out.

"Can I help you?" she asked with trepidation. She was short, black, and had her hair tied up in a tight bun. Rob could see she was the paramedic which meant her partner that was now walking around the ambulance to join them was probably an EMT.

"We saw your rig and wanted to make sure you guys were okay. What are you doing here?" Rob asked.

"Well," the paramedic said, drawing out the word, clearly irritated. "If you haven't noticed, nothing is working, including our ambulance. That's what we are doing here."

Rachel cut in before Rob could reply, "We know nothing is working. What he means is, what are you still doing here? As in why haven't you left? This isn't exactly the best area to be in during the day, let alone when it's dark."

"What are we supposed to do?" the paramedic raised both hands, palms up. She was clearly becoming more and more annoyed, and her voice was becoming louder.

"Umm walk maybe? Your legs still work," Rachel said with her arms crossed while she glared at the paramedic. Rachel was also getting louder.

The EMT, a Hispanic male in his thirties and around Rob's size, was now standing next to Rob, with both of them watching the unfolding confrontation.

"And leave the rig behind?" She slowly rolled her eyes to make sure Rachel and Rob could see how stupid she thought the conversation was. "With all the equipment and meds? You aren't very bright are you? You're outta your damn mind if you think we're abandoning our rig. Someone like you would probably break in and steal everything," Arms now crossed and almost yelling, the paramedic took a step towards Rachel. The EMT was watching and had an amused look on his face. Rob knew he needed to defuse the situation before it became physical.

"Ladies!" Rob yelled. They both stopped and looked at him, Rachel with surprise on her face. "Hold up, listen," Rob said, quieter now that he had their attention. "We got off on the wrong foot and I apologize. My name is Rob, this is Rachel. We work at the dispatch center in Riverside off Alessandro."

At this point the EMT realized what Rob was trying to do and decided to help out. "I'm Miguel, my partner is Jasmine." He stuck out his hand and shook with Rob, then they both turned to the females, Rob holding his hand out to Jasmine, Miguel to Rachel. Both females waited a beat, then shook. They conspicuously did not shake each other's hand. "Pretty crazy what's going on, no?" Miguel added.

"Yeah, end of the world stuff," Rob replied.

"What do you mean, end of the world?" Jasmine asked

"You guys don't have any idea of what's really happening, do you?" Rob asked.

Jasmine just scoffed, as if the idea Rob or Rachel would know anything she didn't was ridiculous, but Miguel asked, "What's really happening? What are you talking about?" He confirmed Rob's suspicion that neither Jasmine nor Miguel had any idea of the seriousness of the situation they found themselves in. Rob could see he had Miguel's rapt attention, and even though Jasmine was doing her best to appear as if the conversation was a waste of time Rob knew she was listening.

"Your ambulance died and the city blacked out at the same time, right?" Rob got nods from both. "Your cell phones working?" Both shook their heads no. "How about any of the equipment in the back?"

"We haven't checked," Jasmine said, sounding a little less annoyed. "We weren't transporting a patient so none of it would be on anyways."

Miguel was already walking to the back doors, followed by Rob, Rachel, and Jasmine. Miguel opened the doors and stepped up into the walkway between the gurney and a bench that was situated against the side of the ambulance. He reached over and held down the power button on what Rob thought was some sort of heart monitor. There was no response from the equipment. "That's weird," he said as he tried two other electronic devices. Again, no response from either. "This should all be working. I checked all of it before we went in service and it was fine. And the one patient we ran to County Hospital was hooked up to two of these and they worked fine. What the heck?"

"Either of you ever see the sky like that?" Rob continued his line of questions.

They both shook their head and Jasmine said, "I've lived here all my life and I've never seen it before. It's an aurora right? Like you see on those nature shows of the north pole."

"That's right." Rob continued, addressing both medical professionals, "You're both smart, you have to be in your line of work. Any of those things I just asked you about could be explained if they happened individually. But they all happened at the same time. The power, your rig, cellphones, the equipment in the back, the aurora. What are the odds of all of that happening at the same time?"

"Okay I get what you are saying, but that doesn't tell us what's going on," Miguel said.

"What I'm going to tell you will probably make me sound like a nut job conspiracy theorist. And to be honest, even though I prepared for it, I always thought it sounded a little far-fetched myself." Rob paused a moment as his mind turned, trying to come up with the quick version. He wanted to get moving again. "I'll start this by saying I don't know all of the science and how it all works, but I do know there are two things that could have caused this, and they both have the same effect. The first is a solar flare, the second is a nuclear device detonated somewhere in the atmosphere. Because of the aurora, and the alerts we received from NAWAS prior to it happening, I'm leaning towards a solar flare, but I could be completely wrong. Anyways, if either of those happen, and they are strong enough, they knock out everything electronic. Basically humanity is set back a couple centuries." Rob stopped to let them digest the information.

"Wait, NAWAS?" Miguel asked, clearly puzzled. Rob gave them both the quick version of what NAWAS was and the two alerts.

"So how long does it last?" Jasmine asked.

"It depends on how fast stuff can be repaired. But think about it. Every single electronic device is going to need repaired. Every single car is going to need replacement parts. And the power grid is the biggest thing. From what I understand the components that will be needed to replace the affected parts of the power grid can take a year or more to make. And if they need hundreds or thousands of those parts it can be years before we have power again. That's if the plants that make the parts even have power themselves."

"C'mon bro, that can't be right. The government has to have contingency plans and backups in place for all of this," Miguel said with disbelief on his face.

"When's the last time the government did anything efficiently?" Rob's question was rhetorical. "The government has known how vulnerable everything is for a long time and they haven't done anything to prepare for it. I guarantee you as soon as they knew how bad it was going to be they all high tailed it for the nearest bunker to try to save themselves. We are on our own."

"That's one of the craziest things I've ever heard," Jasmine retorted with a snort and another exaggerated eye roll. "You have gone off the deep end."

"Told you I'd sound like a nut job. I promise you though no one is coming to help you. My suggestion is for you guys to get your stuff and start walking home. Things are not going to be pretty soon. In fact I think things are going to get very, very ugly, and very soon."

"Man, you are crazy. You belong in the mental ward at County. I thought you dispatchers took psych exams before being hired," Jasmine huffed before turning and walking back to the passenger side of the ambulance. She climbed back into her seat and slammed the door.

Miguel was still standing there, and Rob could see his mind was racing. "How do you know all this stuff?" he asked.

This time Rachel answered, "A bunch of us dispatchers took a terrorism class sponsored by Homeland Security. The guy who gave the class went over this same exact scenario."

Rob took back over, "And after the class I did some of my own research and I'm telling you this is literally the end of the world as we know it. Of course it's your choice, but I really think you should try to make it home."

"Yeah," Miguel said quietly. "I've got some thinking to do."

"We're going to move on. Nice to meet you Miguel," Rob said, once again shaking his hand. "Good luck to both of you."

"Listen, I know she's your partner," Rachel said as she nodded towards the front of the ambulance. "Just don't let her influence your thinking. Rob might sound crazy, but I promise you he's not. Good luck to you," she finished the conversation with her own handshake.

As they walked by the ambulance Rob gave Jasmine a wave and a nod. She shook her head and crossed her arms over her chest. *Too bad. A few days from now she'll probably remember this and wish she had listened to me. Oh well. Too bad I couldn't get any narcotics.* Rob knew there was no way Jasmine would allow him to take anything from the ambulance without putting up a fight, and he wasn't desperate enough to force the issue. Not yet at least.

A few minutes later Rachel started talking. "Hey, sorry about that back there. I almost lost it on that dumbass. Here you are trying to help her out and she's treating you like you're a moron. But, I still should have just shut up."

"No worries. I was looking forward to a chick fight but didn't want to take the time to let you beat her ass. We need to stay on schedule," Rob said with a laugh. His joke worked, causing Rachel to laugh as well and lightening the mood. "Seriously though, she was an asshole. It's fine if she doesn't want to believe it, but she doesn't have to act like that either. I'm hoping she's just scared and will think about what she heard. Oh well, what are you gonna do right?"

"Yeah. Guess we can't save 'em all."

"Yeah. Thanks for backing me up though."

"No problem," Rachel said. "I was surprised when you yelled. I worked with you for five years and never once did I see you even become upset, let alone yell."

"It's not often that I do. She just rubbed me the wrong way. I hope Miguel trusts his instincts and leaves for home even if she wants to stay. He was on the verge of leaving when we did but I think he was worried about leaving her there."

"Yeah hopefully." Rob and Rachel lapsed into silence again as they continued their journey east. They picked up their pace and walked the mile to Heacock Street, through commercial buildings and warehouses without incident, in less than thirty minutes.

A few hundred feet short of Heacock Rob called for another break. "I need to use the restroom again, and we need to take a quick break before we tackle the residential area." They walked into a large grassy field next to the street where they put down their bags. Rob got out his Kershaw Siege and roll of toilet paper, "I'll be right back," and walked over to, and climbed down into, a storm drainage ditch that traversed the length of the field. He used the hatchet to dig a small hole that he used to relieve himself, then covered it up and walked back over to where Rachel was waiting with their bags. "You need to go?" he asked.

"Just pee, I'll be right back." She jumped up with a few napkins she had saved from earlier and walked over to the ditch. She was back within a couple minutes.

"So, this is what I'm thinking," Rob began. "We just keep heading east on Cactus, go straight through as fast as possible. Once we reach Lasselle we'll be out of the housing tracts and back into open fields. Then the only thing we have to worry about is the hospital before we get to your neighborhood. But you live here, so you know the area better than I do. Any other ideas?" Rob asked her.

"No, that sounds good to me. There really isn't a way to go around that doesn't go through neighborhoods, and the good thing is all the houses on cactus face away from the street and into their own neighborhoods. With any luck we'll get through without seeing anyone."

"Yeah that's what I'm hoping, glad we are on the same page. I'm going to down this energy drink," Rob said as he pulled one of the BANG energy drinks from his bag. "We need to move fast, so if you're feeling a little tired you might want to as well." Rob stood up and flexed his knees a few times by squatting down to the ground. Other than a little soreness his knees felt fine. And once the energy drink kicked in he would be good to go. Ten minutes later he stood and put on his backpack and Rachel rose and did the same with her messenger bag. Without a word they walked back to the street, then turned east and headed into the residential neighborhoods of this section of Moreno Valley.

CHAPTER 4

Rob and Rachel walked at a fast pace. Not so fast that they would tire themselves out, but fast enough that Rob hoped they would make it through the two miles of residential area before sunrise. The aurora turned the darkness into twilight, but it was better than walking through in the middle of a bright sunny day. It was 5:30 am so they had about an hour and a half to make the two miles. *Cutting it close,* Rob thought. He wasn't sure they would make it, but they were going to try. If they didn't hit any obstacles on the way through they should make it, but Rob wasn't counting on smooth sailing. The farther they got the better.

Rob elected to walk in the street but close to the curb line. That way they had good fields of view for what was ahead and behind them, but were also close enough to any bushes and trees in the grass area next to the sidewalk that might give them some concealment if needed. At intersections they paused to look up and down each side street to confirm everything was quiet before proceeding across. At T-intersections, where small residential streets let out onto Cactus Avenue but did not continue on the other side, they crossed the street and walked on the opposite side of where the side street let out.

The area they were now in was a series of tract home developments that were built in the 1970's and 80's. On the main streets that ran through the area, the houses all faced away with their backyards facing the main streets, divided from the streets almost exclusively using eight foot block walls. The interior streets that ran through each neighborhood mostly made several turns and had numerous cul-de-sacs placed throughout. The houses were all single-family homes on somewhat small properties with the houses separated by only fifteen feet and a wooden fence. There weren't a lot of trees in the neighborhoods, especially compared to some of the neighborhoods on the other side of the city, but the ones that were there were mature and provided large amounts of shade in the summer. *It wouldn't be a bad place to live, except for the gangs. And if you didn't mind being shoulder to shoulder with your neighbors of course,* Rob thought.

The first obstacle they ran into was at the intersection of Cactus and Perham Drive. Several hundred feet short of the intersection they could hear numerous people talking from up ahead. Rob and Rachel crossed to the right side of the street and stopped. "Wait here, I'm going ahead to check it out. Keep an eye out and scream if you need me to get back here fast. Also, be ready to run in case I'm spotted."

Rachel looked scared but nodded, "Be safe and come right back."

"I will," Rob said with a reassuring smile. So that he would present a smaller profile to anyone who looked in his direction, and he would be a little lighter and faster on his feet if the need arose, he set his Eberlestock backpack just off the sidewalk and next to a bush so that it wasn't readily visible in the bright light of the aurora, then proceeded slowly towards the voices.

He utilized the sidewalk and stayed close to the cinder block wall that separated the street from the backyards of the houses next to them. When he was even with the corner house, but still several dozen feet short of the intersection, he could see light from a fire coming from the right. He moved slowly and quietly ahead until he could see across the front yard of the house. Unfortunately, due to a large tree and cars parked in the driveway of the house he was next to he couldn't see anything other than the glow of the fire. Rob got down on his hands and knees and crawled through the front yard, using the tree and cars as cover. He made it to the tree, stood up, and peaked around, and found his view still obstructed by the cars in the driveway. He could see some movement and shadows but not enough to get a good handle on what was going on. He got back down and crawled to the cars, trying as best he could to watch his surroundings. He reached the cars and from a crouched position slowly peaked over the trunk of a white four door sedan.

Across the street, in the second house from Cactus, he has visual of about fifteen males and females. They were mostly gathered around a large bon fire they had started in the drive-way of the house, and most had obviously been drinking. If it had been just the group around the bon fire Rob would have felt comfortable trying to sneak past, knowing the campfire was playing havoc with their night vision and they were engrossed in whatever conversation that was taking place. Unfortunately, there were also four males in the street shooting hoops through a portable basketball hoop, and with the night still brighter than normal due to the aurora, there was a good chance they would spot Rob and Rachel if they attempted to cross the inter-section.

As Rob watched he caught snippets of the conversation. He caught the words cops, hood, crips, bloods, and power. It was obvious they were members of one of the local gangs hav-ing an impromptu meeting, but other than those words Rob couldn't figure out what specifically they were talking about. He watched for a few more seconds then crawled backwards until he was at the corner of the house. Once he was certain he was out of the group's line of sight he stood up and quietly made his way back to Rachel.

He told her what he found, "Bad news. Almost twenty people, gangsters I think, with a bon fire. No way we can sneak past them. We'll have to double back and go around them. You know this area better than me, which way do you think is better?"

Rachel thought about it for a minute. "If we go north to Brodiaea we are going to have to cut through the neighborhood, and I don't think there is a street that goes straight through, so we would end up walking up and down several side streets. If we go south to Delphinium, we can use the street we just passed, it goes straight through, then we can go down Delphinium and cut through Badger Springs Middle School and the elementary school that's next to it, then through the fields back to Cactus."

"Okay that's what we'll do then," Rob said as he picked up his backpack and put it on. They backtracked west until they came to Joshua Tree Avenue. He could see that it did in fact cut straight through to Delphinium Avenue. and he took a long look at both sides of the street to make sure everything was quiet. Once he was happy nothing was moving he told Rachel, "Let's move quick and get over to Delphinium. Keep a real good eye out," then started walking fast.

They walked along the left curb line even though most of the houses faced them. On the right side of the street only a few houses faced the street, but there were three side streets to cross on that side. The other advantage to the left side was there were a lot more cars parked on the curb than there was on the right side; cars they could take cover behind if they needed to. They walked quickly, both scanning back and forth left and right, with Rob doing his usual backwards walk to occasionally take a good look behind them. At one point while looking around Rob noticed Rachel had her ASP in her hand ready to go. *Smart girl,* he thought. During the entire walk to Delphinium they both felt like a thousand eyes were watching them from the windows of the houses, but they made it without incident.

Before making the left turn onto Delphinium they paused to check both directions. While they checked Rob asked Rachel, "How far down is that school? A few blocks, right?"

"I think its four, but it's not far."

"You good to jog? I want to make it there as fast as possible."

"Oh yeah, let's do it," she replied.

"Okay, real quick, make sure nothing you have is going to make any noise as we run. Once we start moving, other than clearing intersections, let's try to make it all the way there without stopping. We can take a break once we reach the school."

After a quick look in her bag Rachel took some of the slack out of the shoulder strap so it rode a little higher. This way she could keep better control of the bag and it wouldn't bounce around so much as they jogged down the street. She looked at Rob with a determined look on her face and gave him a nod, indicating that she was ready.

They set out at a quick jog, utilizing the right side of the street this time. When they reached the first intersection, Perham, they paused to check left and right. To the left they could see the same group that had caused them to detour in the first place, but they were far enough away that Rob felt confident they could cross without catching the attention of the large group. To the right was only darkness and quiet. Crouching to reduce their profile, they moved as fast as possible to the east side of the street. Once across they hid behind a parked car and watched the group for a minute to make sure they had not been spotted. With no change in the group's activities they started out again, still on the right side of the street to avoid the small residential cross streets on the left.

They were making good time and were just short of a side street which let out of the neighborhood on the left when Rob came to an abrupt stop. Rachel, not reacting fast enough to Rob's sudden lack of motion, ran right into his back. "What's going on? Why'd you stop?" she asked in a whisper.

"I thought I heard something, like a banging sound. I think it's coming from that side street. Let's slow down and use these cars to get where we can see down that street before we cross." Together they crouched behind the cars, moving slowly and stopping at each gap in the parked vehicles to try to get a visual down the side street. They were even with the side street and were behind a large dark blue pick-up truck and still could not see anything. There was a gap of about five car lengths to the next parked car due to the driveways of two houses being next to each other at that point of the street. After a minute of looking and listening Rob started to wonder if his mind was playing tricks on him.

"I'm going to go first," Rob told Rachel. "You keep a good eye on the street. Once I'm across and behind that next car I'll wave you over when it's your turn. When you move don't hesitate and get across fast."

"Okay I'm ready," she replied.

Rob was about to make his move when movement caught his eye. "Hold up, check it out," he whispered to Rachel, while pointing down the side street. "Right side, about two thirds of the way down next to that white mini-van." They could now see what was making the noise. Someone was on the sidewalk holding a large stick or pole. As they watched he walked into the street, moved to the driver side door of the mini-van, and used the stick to smash out the driver side window. He reached inside and unlocked the door, then pulled it open and got inside. They could see him moving around inside the van and Rob figured he was searching for anything he deemed valuable. The thief was done in less than forty-five seconds, got out and started walking to the next vehicle. They watched as he walked around the car, this time a silver sedan, and tried each door handle. When he wasn't successful in finding an unlocked door, he moved over to the passenger front door.

"Rachel, have you seen anyone except him?" he asked, whispering.

"No," she whispered back while shaking her head no.

"Okay, when he gets into the car we are both going to move together, quick as possible. Once we move we are going to keep moving. Let's get outta his line of site in case he hops out and looks this way. Ready?" This time she nodded, still wearing the look of determination on her face.

They watched as the thief smashed the passenger window, reached inside and unlocked the door, then pulled it open and got inside. As soon as he was starting to get into the car Rob tapped Rachel on the shoulder and took off running down the sidewalk with Rachel right behind him.

They reached the intersection of Delphinium and Indian Street and could now see the school that was their destination. They took a good look up and down Indian before making their way across. Once across they jogged into the parking lot of Badger Springs Middle School and up to the main entrance. The school was fenced all the way around but near the main entrance they found a short stucco wall with a small rod iron fence on top of it. The wall made getting over easy, so they tossed their bags over then scrambled over themselves.

Once onto the school grounds Rob told Rachel, "Start making your way towards the back of the school and take a quick look around. I'm going to wait here a minute and make sure no one is following us. I wasn't able to watch our back really well while we were running over here. I don't think that guy smashing car windows saw us but better safe than sorry," *I also need to catch my breath,* he didn't add. *I really should have done more cardio.* "Just don't go to where we can't see or hear each other."

"Okay," Rachel replied before making her way into the school.

Rob waited about three minutes and was happy to see the area they just came from was still and quiet. By this time Rachel was walking back to him, "I checked just past this building. It leads into a center courtyard of some sort. I took a good look there and I didn't hear or see anyone."

"Good work, lets head that way." They walked together through the buildings. "Keep your eye open for broken windows or doors that have been forced open. There's been a group of dummies breaking into schools in Moreno Valley for the past month or so and they haven't been caught. It would suck to run into them right now." They walked into the courtyard and Rob changed his mind. "Instead of continuing let's take advantage of the privacy we have here. The buildings block anyone from seeing us from outside the school and we should be able to hear someone walking up before they seen us. We can take a short break."

"That sounds good to me," Rachel replied as she put her messenger bag onto an outdoor table normally used by the students of the school. "I really need to pee again. This is way too much excitement for me."

After looking around Rob could only see one option to relieve themselves without leaving the courtyard. Unfortunately it had no cover. "See that small section of dirt in the corner of that building?" Rachel nodded as Rob pointed. "Use that to go and I'll stand watch."

"Okay, just no looking," Rachel said with a chuckle.

"Wouldn't think of it, cross my heart hope to die, or pinky promise, or whatever the kids are saying nowadays," he said with amusement in his voice.

After Rachel did her business, she stood watch for Rob while he did the same. Then they sat at the table and drank some water and ate a protein bar each. "What do you think you'll do afterwards?" Rachel asked, curiosity in her voice.

"Well after this I'm going to get you home, then go home my-self," not realizing she was referencing the long term.

"No, I mean after after. Like once everything calms down, a year or five years from now," she explained.

"Ah," Rob said, finally grasping what she was asking. He thought for a minute before answering. "You know, I've never really thought about that. Anytime I thought about an end of the world scenario or major disaster and what I would do in re-sponse, my focus was always on the initial surviving. Surviving the first night, then the first week, and the first few months. I've never thought long term." Rob fell silent again as he pondered the question.

Finally, he continued, "Of course, my main priority is making sure my family lives through the initial chaos that the EMP is going to cause. Then to make sure they live long term in what I'm sure will be a new normal. I really do think the power is going to be off for a very long time, and by the time things are calmed down enough to start repairing the damage I'm not sure if there will be anyone left alive to actually do the repairs. That's a deep question, and I guess my answer right now is, other than surviving, I don't really know. What about you?"

"I'm in the same boat as you. Or maybe a worse boat. I've never even planned for a disaster like an earthquake, let alone the end of the world. I have no clue." They both fell into a silence as they contemplated the long term outlook for both of their families.

After another five minutes it was time to go. They shouldered their bags and started walking, continuing north through the courtyard then making a right turn next to what looked like a large enclosure with several dumpsters inside. On the left was a large open asphalt area with several basketball courts separated from the area they were currently in by a short fence. They walked to the end of the fence where there was an opening next to a building, went through the opening, made a right to continue east through the school grounds, and came to a sudden stop.

Rob and Rachel had almost walked directly into three people. A Hispanic guy with numerous tattoos on his arms, neck, and shaved head which Rob was almost certain were mostly prison tattoos wearing a green shirt with an eagle on it and blue jeans carrying a crowbar. Another Hispanic guy wearing a black hoodie and black skinny jeans carrying a bat. The third was a black guy wearing a red hoodie and blue jeans also carrying a bat. All three were around five feet ten inches with average builds, but what mostly concerned Rob were the weapons they were carrying. *Well at least I'm a little better armed. Nothing like bringing a stick to a gunfight. Unless one of them has a gun that I can't see of course,* Rob thought.

"Well, what do we have here?" the Hispanic guy with green shirt and crowbar said. "Looks like these two love birds are trespassing on school grounds."

"Look guys," Rob said. "We're just passing through. How about you just let us through, then you can go back to whatever it was you were doing before we showed up, and no one will get hurt tonight." He knew anything short of being tough towards them would just make them think he was weak and easy prey.

"I think he just threatened us guys. Looks like they gots some good stuff too," the black guy with the red hoodie said, looking sideways at his friends. He then looked directly at Rachel, "Drop your bag honey, I'll make this painless for you."

As all three started to move closer Rob had his gun out and pointed at the head of the closest one, which turned out to be the Hispanic guy wearing the black skinny jeans with the bat, in less than a second. This caused all three to stop dead in their tracks.

"Like I was saying, just let us pass through and none of you will get hurt," Rob said. "Now, drop your sticks and turn around. I'm not screwin' around with you guys."

"You ain't gonna shoot no one dude," green shirt with the crowbar said. "Bet you the gun ain't even loaded."

Rob moved the gun so that it was pointed at green shirt with the crowbars' head, "You die first." No one moved or spoke for about twenty seconds. "What's it going to be?" Rob asked staring green shirt in the eyes. "Either we walk away, and you guys go about your business, or we walk away after you all die. Either way, we walk away." The first to drop his bat was red hoodie, followed closely by black hoodie. Green shirt had fury in his eyes and was shaking with anger, but after a few more seconds he dropped the crowbar. *If any of them try anything it'll be him. He's pissed,* Rob thought. "Now turn around, face the building and get on your knees. Count slowly to one hundred before you get up. If you follow us I promise it will end badly for you."

"Man fuck you, homie," green shirt said. "You ain't doin' shit. Soon as you gone we gonna catch up to you and make you watch while we fuck yo girl. Then we gonna kill you nice and slow."

"You aren't fucking anyone. You touch me, and you'll regret it," Rachel said quietly, with a hardness in her voice. Rob was surprised, but knew she meant every word.

"Screw you bitch," Green shirt continued, now looking Rachel up and down with a lascivious look on his face. "I'm gonna do stuff to you that you wouldn't never think of. And it's gonna hurt. You're gonna-."

Rob didn't let him finish. He pointed the gun at green shirt's stomach and pulled the trigger. He didn't bother to aim, knowing that taking the time to line up the sights and obtain a proper sight picture was a waste of time. From three feet away all he needed to do was point the gun and pull the trigger and he was all but guaranteed to hit his target. Once he pulled the trigger Rob immediately moved his gun to cover the other two in case they decided to rush him. Green shirt immediately stopped talking, covered his stomach, and had a puzzled look on his face. It took him a few seconds to realize he had been shot, then he stumbled back a few steps until his back hit the wall of the building and he slid down into a sitting position.

"The fuck, man!" screamed red hoodie while black hoodie got down on his knees trying to render aid to his cohort.

Rob raised his voice, "All of you shut the hell up! I told you I wasn't screwing around. I swear to you, if you follow us you're gonna go out like your friend. Do you understand me?"

"Yeah man, just get the fuck outta here!" black hoodie screamed.

Rob started backing up with Rachel right next to him. He could see she looked terrified. "Keep moving," he said in a loud whisper.

Rob walked quickly backwards until they hit the field just east of the basketball courts, then they turned and ran. Once they reached the fence that separated the two schools' fields they quickly scaled it, not bothering to take off their bags as the fence was chain link and only four feet high, and continued to run, with Rob continuously checking behind them to make sure the two uninjured criminals weren't following.

They reached the fence that divided the elementary school property from the open field next to it, another four feet high chain link fence, and quickly jumped it as well, then ran flat out in a northeast direction across the field. They reached the corner of the intersection of Perris Boulevard and Cactus and paused. "Check the streets all four directions, let me know if you see anything," Rob said as he studied the field and school behind them for movement. After twenty seconds neither saw anything that caused them concern, so they crossed Perris at a run and continued east on Cactus.

They continued to run flat out, only stopping briefly at side streets to check for movement, until they reached Kitching Street. At this point Rob stopped. "Hold up, lets catch our breath," he said between deep breaths. Stopping here wasn't the best idea due to still being in the middle of heavily populated areas, but he needed to catch his breath and check their rear to make sure they weren't being followed.

"There is a park up ahead, one more block on the right, we can rest there," Rachel suggested. She was barely breathing hard whereas Rob was huffing and puffing.

"You a runner or something?" He asked her.

"Not much anymore, but I ran track in high school, and still try to run a few miles at least once a week."

"No wonder I can't keep up with you, I'm racing a friggin' track star." Rob said as he made one more quick check behind, then in both directions on Kitching. "Okay, let's go. Keep an eye out as we move. We'll rest at the park."

They crossed Kitching and moved at a much slower, but still quick pace down Cactus. They were both eager to get out of the residential area. They reached Woodland Park on the right and found a small stand of young oak trees towards the south end of the park. "Let's rest here. Five minutes, then we go. We only have a couple blocks until we reach the open fields."

"Okay," Rachel agreed as they walked into the trees, took off their bags, and sat down, using the trees as cover. The benches and picnic tables in the park were too exposed to use, especially with the park being right in the middle of a neighborhood, surrounded on all sides by houses. Rachel immediately took out a water bottle and started drinking heavily from it.

As Rob started rehydrating himself he noticed Rachel had a faraway look in her eyes. "You okay?" he asked her gently, knowing what she witnessed had to be traumatic for her.

"Yeah... I just... I...," she stuttered at first, then in a rush said, "I can't believe that actually happened. I can't believe you shot that guy. Why'd you shoot him?"

Rob took a moment to gather his thoughts before speaking. "I didn't want to shoot him, but I want to get home more. The way he threatened to follow us, the way he threatened to rape you then kill me, we couldn't take the chance that they would actually try to do it. If they did try, there is no way of knowing if next time they would get the jump on us. If they did surprise us, then we would never make it home to our families. He brought it on himself and I'll sleep like a baby knowing he didn't turn us into victims and he won't victimize anyone else in the future."

After a minute or so Rachel finally responded, "Yeah I guess you're right. It's just... as much as I think about it, as much as I believe you did the right thing to get us home, I never would have thought that not only would I see something like that happen but also be friends with the guy who did it."

"That's totally understandable," Rob replied. "Trust me, I didn't want to do it. I don't like what I did. What I do like is that we are both still alive. That you aren't raped and left for dead. That I'm not dead after being tortured. That we are both living to fight another day. If I thought for a second that those dirt bags would have left us alone once we walked away I wouldn't have done it. But the look in his eyes... you could tell he wasn't going to give up. He would chase me all the way to Yucaipa if he had to. Did you notice the tattoos?" Rachel nodded, and Rob continued, "I'm pretty sure most of them were prison tats. He did some serious time at some point to have all that. And I'm not an expert, but I think he was a gang member based on a couple of them that I could see. With someone like that, respect is one of the most important things they hold onto. Especially in front of their fellow gangsters. They feel disrespected and it's worth killing over and I couldn't let that happen to us. If he felt disrespected in front of his friends, he would have to do something to us to maintain credibility."

Another moment of silence passed while Rachel battled with her own emotions. Finally, she spoke, sounding worn out, "I get it, and I'm grateful for what you did. I really am. This new world is just going to take some getting used to, that's all."

"You just have to focus on your family. I keep saying the world is different now and I mean that. The only thing that matters is your own safety and the safety of your family. As much as I hate it, I'm sure there is going to be a lot more death before this is all said and done. And for what it's worth, you did a great job. There was no doubt in my mind that he would regret touching you."

They both fell silent and Rob decided to replace the single round of ammo he expended during their confrontation with the hooligans at the school. First, Rob drew his gun and pulled one of the full magazines from the holder on his belt. Second, he dropped the magazine from the gun, replaced it with the full one, and holstered the gun. Next, he pulled the box of ammo out of his backpack, took a round out, inserted it into the magazine he had removed from the gun, and put the now full magazine into the magazine holder on his belt. After a few minutes Rob stood back up. "Let's go, almost there."

As they walked through the park back towards Cactus they both stopped. They could hear screaming and yelling and it sounded like it was coming from the northeast area of the park. Right in the area they were about to walk through. As Rob listened he thought it was at least two males and three females and it sounded like they were in a serious fight. He wasn't sure as it was hard to make out what was being said but it sounded like one of the females was saying something about putting a knife down and one of the males was threatening to get a gun from a car. *Another issue. Can't we just catch a break? This is exhausting*, Rob thought to himself.

"Let's go the other way. We can try to cut through the neighborhood and get back to Delphinium," Rob said. They both turned and started walking quickly south through the park. They cut through to the southeast side of the park, passing playgrounds and a baseball diamond, before coming out onto White Wood Circle. Not being familiar with the area Rob only knew Delphinium was to the south but not which streets they needed to take to get there, so once again he deferred to Rachel's more intimate knowledge of the area. "Which way?" he asked her.

"To the right. I think we just need to follow it where it turns left then use the little side street about halfway down to come out to Delphinium." Rob was happy to hear some of the determination and hardness was making its way back into her voice.

"Okay, back through the houses then. Eyes and ears open. Let's go." They went south to where the street took a sudden ninety degree left turn and changed names from White Wood to Figwood Way. Jogging the whole way they passed a cul-de-sac then came out to Rosemary Avenue which they used to head south and reach Delphinium again. After they walked the one block south and checked both directions on Delphinium they turned east and jogged to Lasselle. The intersection of Lasselle and Delphinium was a T-intersection. The west side of Lasselle on both sides of Delphinium was residential with numerous tract home neighborhoods. The east side of Lasselle was a large field covering almost 400 acres. At some point in the past large sections were graded for future neighborhoods that were never built due to the 2008 economic depression that severely affected the housing industry.

At the intersection they both looked both directions, then crossed at a run. They moved straight into the field, electing to use it as cover so they could rest and also knowing that the hospital was just to the north. They came to a cattle fence and Rob made a small opening big enough to crawl through by stepping and pushing down on the lowest barbed wire and at the same time pulling up on the middle one. "Pass your bag through then go through yourself, then do the same for me." Rachel complied, and Rob was quickly through himself. They jogged several hundred feet into the field until they reached the first rise and dip in the terrain.

"I'm going to check behind us to make sure no one is following. You scout ahead and find somewhere we can rest. Make sure it's in a spot that can't be seen from the houses," Rob said. He knelt and studied the neighborhood they just left, watching for movement.

"Got it," Rachel replied as she walked further east. Rob waited several minutes before deciding it was long enough, then got up and followed Rachel. He moved a couple hundred yards through the field before he heard her, just off to his left. "Hey over here Rob."

Rob found her in a slight depression that was flat and clear of brush and holes, but more importantly out of the line of sight of the surrounding areas. "Good job, this spot is perfect," he told her.

Drained of energy they both took off their bags, collapsed onto the hard ground, and rested.

CHAPTER 5

Rob and Rachel laid on the ground for about twenty minutes before he noticed the sky was starting to get lighter. After checking his watch, he told Rachel, "It's 6:55. Let's rest for another thirty minutes or so before we make the last push to your neighborhood."

"Good idea," she responded. "I'm exhausted." Rob could hear it in her voice and was sure he sounded just as tired.

"It's the adrenaline dump combined with all the stress. It's an exhausting combination." Rob took off his shoes and socks and started rubbing his sore feet. While the Merrell hiking shoes were comfortable to walk in, they weren't exactly the best footwear to run in. Fortunately, once he left Rachel's neighborhood most of his journey would be through mainly rural ranch and farm land, with a few smaller neighborhoods to navigate in Moreno Valley, until he reached his own city of Yucaipa. Rob draped the socks over his shoes to let them dry out while they rested. He also decided to take some more ibuprofen. His knees weren't hurting too bad, but he wanted to make sure they didn't get any worse before making the final push.

Rob took out his canteen and between drinks asked Rachel, "Hey, you're sure your husband is home?"

"On my last break last night, before everything went to hell, we talked on the phone. He said after he got off work he stopped at my mom's house and picked up our daughter and went straight home, made dinner then started getting her ready for bed after they ate. The last thing he texted me was that she was asleep, and he was in bed. That was around 10:00 or so."

"That's good. Question for you: when we get to your place, if it's okay with you and your husband of course, would you mind if I rested up for the rest of the day? I'll leave sometime around dark. Feel free to say no, you won't offend me. I'll understand if you would rather I not."

Rachel snorted as if the question was ridiculous, "Don't be stupid. Of course you can stay. Stay as long as you need to. Carlos, my husband, won't mind. Especially when I tell him what we've been through."

"Thank you," Rob replied with obvious relief. He would rather keep going, but knew he needed to rest. If he kept pushing himself, he would eventually collapse from exhaustion and never make it home. They spent the rest of their break eating, rehydrating, and telling each other about their families. Rachel's husband, Carlos, worked a Monday through Friday, eight to five job as the manager overseeing obtaining new contracts for a local construction company. He had worked for the company since he was twenty-four and worked his way up from a journeyman electrician, to a lead electrician, to a site foreman, and finally to his current position. Rachel's daughter was Samantha, "A sassy three years old going on fifteen," as Rachel described her. It was good to be able to sit and talk, almost as if everything was normal again. *Except for the fact that they were in the middle of a field. After having walked half the night through the city. And breaking into a gas station. And almost being attacked by a dog. And shooting a guy and threatening his friends with their lives. Yeah, normal, except for all that,* Rob thought to himself sarcastically.

They ended up trading stories of their families and resting for almost an hour before Rob checked his watch again. 7:44 am. "Last push. Let's get up before we fall asleep right here," he said as he began putting his socks and shoes back on. Rachel gathered up all her stuff before wearily getting to her feet and putting her messenger bag over her shoulder. Before putting on his own backpack he took the Oakley sunglasses out of his backpack and put them on. They would be walking directly into the rising sun.

Rachel stared at Rob for a minute before taking a quick look through her bag. "Dang it, I left my sunglasses in my car," she said while shaking her head. "Oh well, almost there. Just a little bit longer and we can get some real rest."

As they started walking east through the field Rob said, "Let's just stay in the field. I want to avoid the hospital as much as possible. There's no telling what the situation is over there. The power has been out almost eight hours now and people are going to start getting desperate. I'm sure it's becoming a living hell in there."

They walked through the field, taking an hour to cover just three quarters of a mile, their progress slowed by the uneven terrain, numerous gopher holes, and brush that hadn't been cleared in quite some time. They were getting close to the end of the large open lot when they crested a small rise and looking north they could see the hospital. Rob's instincts had been correct. There was a large crowd near the front entrance, maybe one hundred to one hundred and fifty people, many pushing wheelchairs or holding up family or friends that needed medical care. A line of ten security guards were doing their best to hold them back but starting to fail.

Rob and Rachel watched in horror as one man in the crowd threw a glass bottle towards the guards. He didn't hit anyone, but the crowd became emboldened by the action and started to press forward. The security guards backed up until their backs were pressing against the glass windows and doors that comprised the front entrance of the hospital. One guard, deciding his own well-being was more important than attempting to keep the crowd out of the building, suddenly tried to dart away. He was horrifically unsuccessful as the crowd, now more a mob than anything, grabbed him and started to take their frustrations out on the poor security guard.

Rob watched sadly as the mob beat the guard unconscious, then turned their attention on the other guards. By this time the other guards realized they were no longer going to be able to accomplish their assigned task of keeping the people out of the hospital, and one by one quickly slipped through the partially opened front door. Once they were through the sliding door was pushed shut again. This only held the mob back for another minute or two before three people in the crowd used a metal bench like a battering ram against one of the glass front windows. They hit the window and caused a spiderweb effect on it but didn't completely take it out. It didn't matter, the mob made short work of the glass and by this time the front doors were also being destroyed, completely ripped off their hinges and pushed into the lobby.

The mob entered the hospital with anger in their hearts and Rob did not want to imagine the mayhem they would cause on the inside. And this was only the main entrance to the hospital. He wondered what it was like on the opposite side of the hospital where the emergency department was located.

Rob shook his head in disgust. What did these people hope to accomplish? Yes, they wanted medical care, either for themselves or a loved one, but they knew as well as Rob that the power was out. What kind of services would the hospital be able to offer? Yes, they had the means to administer medications via injections, but in most modern hospital all narcotics and expensive medications, basically anything what was not considered over the counter, was kept under lock and key and the staff would need power to operate the lockers to obtain the medications. Maybe in their anger they would just pull everything from the walls and rip it open until they found what they wanted. It would be little solace in the long run though as without trucks to move supplies from factories and warehouses to hospitals they were only delaying the inevitable.

Rob turned to Rachel, "On the other side of this field, is there a street that cuts through and goes to your house?"

"Yes," Rachel replied, a look on her face that conveyed both sadness and horror. The events they witnessed and were part of during their journey had them both emotionally and mentally depleted. "Delphinium starts up again and cuts through the neighborhood next to mine. But it doesn't go all the way through. At Oliver it turns into Rockwood, Rockcrest, something like that. It doesn't go all the way through, but the street it ties into lets out onto Moreno Beach. My house is right there."

"That's the plan then. I don't want to go anywhere near that hospital, and these neighborhoods coming up don't have the same gang and drug problems that the ones we passed through earlier. That and the sun now being out, I'm sure we can make it through with no problems." They both turned and continued their trek east.

"If that's any indication of what's to come, we are in for a hell of a time," Rachel contemplated as they walked.

"You got that right. And it's only been like eight hours since the EMP. Can you imagine what it's going to look like in twenty-four hours? Or forty-eight hours? Or when people start running out of food? Most stores only hold something like three days of stock in their storage areas, relying on almost daily deliveries to keep the shelves full. And starvation makes people do some horrific things. Especially people with kids. If someone thinks that they can keep their kids alive another day, then most people will do just about anything to make that happen. This world is quickly going down the toilet."

It took another twenty minutes of trudging through, over,

and around heavy brush, holes, and mounds of dirt before they reached the east end of the field and found a fence blocking their progress. This time it was a woven barbed wire fence, no way were they going to be able to use the same technique to get out as they did to get in. They walked south along the fence line until they were even with the T-intersection where Delphinium started up again off Nason Street. Here they found a standard six-foot-high chain link gate. It was chained and padlocked closed but there was enough slack in the chain that Rob was able to move the gate enough to create a foot and a half opening in the middle of the two swinging sections of the gate. Rachel squeezed through first and Rob passed both their bags through, then followed. Due to his larger frame it was a bit of a tight squeeze, but he was soon through and picking up his Eberlestock backpack.

They double checked their surroundings then crossed Nason and started walking east once again on Delphinium. At first, on their right, there was an open field and on the left were tract homes. Soon, Delphinium curved left and they entered an area with houses on both sides. Rob was exhausted but kept up a vigilant watch. They reached the intersection of Delphinium and Oliver Street and stopped to check all directions. On the southeast corner there was another school. This one La Jolla Elementary. "We can stop and rest if you need," Rob suggested.

"Nope, I'm almost home, we are pushing straight through," she replied while shaking her head no to emphasize her point. After what they endured during the night Rachel was in the final stretch before reaching home. Rob knew his answer would be the same if the roles were reversed.

They crossed Oliver and entered Rockwood Avenue, the street name changing from Delphinium at this point. They walked without being confronted by anyone, though Rob was sure he could see curtains being gently moved at several houses, no doubt by homeowners concerned about who might be walking through their neighborhood during a time like this. They walked to the end of Rockwood, stopping at side streets to check their surroundings, Rob occasionally walking backwards, until the street took a sudden ninety degree right turn and changed names once again to Shady Valley Way. They walked south for a few minutes to Auburn Lane, which allowed them to head east again to Moreno Beach Drive. This was a major street that ran through the city, with three lanes in both directions and a large dividing island in the middle.

"How much further is your house?" Rob asked.

"See that large house with the gray tile roof?" Rachel asked, pointing. He could hear the anticipation in her voice. "That's my house." As tired as she was, the weariness in her voice had been replaced with excitement.

Rachel turned right at Moreno Beach with Rob following and she started to pick up her pace. He almost told her to slow down but stopped himself. *She's anxious to get home, I'm not going to slow her down now.* He followed as she made a left onto Artisan Street where she broke into a jog which quickly turned into a run. Her house turned out to be the first one on the left, right where the street made a ninety degree right turn. Her house was a large tan stucco two story which backed up to a flood control channel that helped drain water off the golf course during the heavy rains that sometimes swept through the area.

By the time Rob reached the sidewalk in front of the house Rachel was at the front door trying to put her house key in the lock while simultaneously yelling for her husband. "Carlos! Carlos it's me! I'm home!" She managed to get the dead bolt unlocked and started working on the door knob when the door flew open and a large Hispanic man threw his arms around Rachel and lifted her off her feet in a bear hug. Rob waited respectfully at the sidewalk while they both disappeared into the house.

As he waited Rob studied the house and neighborhood

around him. The house was tan, two stories, and had two drive-ways at the front with one leading to the three-car garage and the other leading around the side of the house. In the side drive-way was a large white enclosed trailer hooked up to a newer model diesel pickup truck with a company logo on the side. The neighborhood was newer, with all the houses being on some-what large properties and having well maintained lawns. As he looked Rob started putting together a basic plan of defense for the house and neighborhood, his plan being to give his ideas to Rachel and Carlos if they wanted it.

It was about five minutes, which Rob was sure was filled with happy tears and joy, before the front door opened again and Rachel waved him over while wiping her eyes with a tissue. "Sorry about that. I should have better manners. Rob this is my husband Carlos, Carlos this is Rob. He's my boss at dispatch."

"Seriously Rachel, you don't need to apologize. I probably would've done the same thing," Rob said as he extended his hand to Carlos. "Nice to meet you Carlos." Up close Rob could see just how big Carlos was. He had to be at least six feet four inches and close to two hundred and fifty pounds, almost none of it fat. He was huge compared to Rob.

Carlos had a glint in his eye as he gave Rob a firm handshake, "Nice to meet you too man, c'mon in, I know you have to be tired. Rachel said you guys walked all night to get here." The happiness was evident in his voice.

"Yeah, it's been a long one," Rob replied tiredly as he stepped into the house.

"Rachel mentioned you staying here a little while to rest up before you take off for home," Rob just nodded. "You can stay as long as you need, mi casa es tu casa. Follow me upstairs and I'll get you set up in our guest room."

Rob followed Carlos into a large guest room equipped with a

queen size bed. It was as if seeing the bed had a physical effect on Rob. He suddenly felt an exhaustion deep in his bones. "I really appreciate it Carlos. I promise it won't be for any longer than necessary. If you don't mind I'm going to clean up as much as I can then get some sleep. Once I wake up we can chat some more."

"Absolutely buddy," Carlos replied. "That door there leads to a bathroom you can use but the water pressure is way down, so I haven't been using the toilets. Other than that, if you need anything just let me know, I'll be downstairs."

"Thanks man, I appreciate it." Rob walked into the bathroom as Carlos left and closed the bedroom door behind him. In the bathroom Rob found some baby wipes. *Perfect, I can clean some of this stink off me.* He stripped out of his clothing and used a few wipes to clean himself as best he could then from his backpack he removed some clean underwear, socks, jeans, and a shirt.

When he was done he left the bathroom, put on the clean underwear, put the rest of the clean clothes and his belt with the holster, knife, and magazines on the dresser, and put his dirty clothes and backpack on the floor in front of the dresser. The Springfield XD he put the nightstand next to the bed. The last thing he did was take off his watch. It was 9:03 am. He placed his watch next to the gun and collapsed onto the bed. It had taken them about nine hours to make it to Rachel's house, but in some ways, it felt like an eternity. As he faded into a deep sleep his thoughts turned to his own family. He said a quick prayer for them before his body finally submitted to the slumber it so desperately needed.

Rob fell into one of those deep sleeps where your dreams feel like real life and time has no meaning. He dreamed of his family and relived some of the trips they had taken. First him and his wife, then with Jackson after she gave birth. Except the trips in his dreams were all mashed up and made no sense.

When Rob woke up it took him a few minutes of looking

around and trying to get his bearings to remember where he was at. When he spotted his watch and gun on the nightstand it all came crashing back to him.

He laid there for a few minutes reveling in the blissful dreams when he realized he could smell coffee. That got him moving. The first thing he did was check his feet again. They were sore, but had no blisters or anything serious so he got up and put on the clean clothes from the top of the dresser, put the holster, magazine holder, and Gerber knife back onto his belt, buckled it, and holstered the gun. He would have left it as he didn't feel the need to have it with him while in the house, but there was no where he could see to keep it secure, and with a little kid running around the house he wouldn't risk an accident. He picked up his watch and strapped it on. 4:12 pm. He'd been asleep for a solid seven hours and felt almost human again. It was amazing what a little sleep could do for a person. He flexed his knees a few times. Sore, but manageable. He left the bag with his dirty clothes on the ground and made his way out of the bedroom then down the stairs, following the smell of coffee.

He walked into the kitchen where he found Rachel and Carlos sitting at the large oak dining table talking quietly and sipping coffee. "Good morning," Rob said by way of greeting with a smile.

"Good afternoon," Carlos replied chuckling. "Coffee?"

"I would do just about anything for a cup of that right now, but first, where can I relieve myself?" Rob asked.

Carlos pointed at a French door at the other end of the kitchen, "That goes into the backyard, I've been using the corner off to the right."

"I'll be right back." Rob walked out, found the correct corner, and did his business. As he walked back to the house he took a better look at the backyard. It was surrounded by a six foot block wall with a wood pedestrian that let out to an open area behind the house. It was several thousand square feet, most of it grass, and had a built in bar-b-que and fire pit with a large Jacuzzi on a concrete slab next to the house.

When Rob walked back into the house Rachel had a cup of coffee ready for him. He noticed they were using a Coleman camp stove powered by small propane bottles and an old school percolator to make their coffee. He was pleased to see they had the stove set up on a table directly under an open window as it would allow any fumes to vent outside while they used it.

"All we have is black, no cream or sugar," she said apologetically.

"That's good by me, beggars can't be choosers." With a smile he took the offered coffee cup and savored the first sip. "Oh man that's good."

"How'd you sleep?" Rachel asked.

"Like a rock. I feel almost normal. You get any sleep?"

"I just got up about an hour ago. I slept hard." A small girl sauntered into the kitchen from the direction of the living room. "Samantha, this is Rob," Rachel introduced her daughter.

Rob got down on one knee so that he was on Samantha's level and put his hand out, "Hi Samantha, it's very nice to meet you. You're even prettier than your momma said you were." Samantha just giggled as she shook his hand.

"Hey Rob," Carlos said as Rob stood back up. "Rachel has been telling me about how you guys made it here from the dispatch center. She told me you went out of your way to walk with her here, and how you handled those guys at the school," he got up from the table and held out his hand. "Thanks for getting her home safe bro, I could never repay you for what you did." Rob could hear the emotion in Carlos' voice and Rob knew he would feel the same way if it was Carlos getting Monica home safe.

"Hey no problem man," Rob replied, shaking Carlos' hand. "If I had known this coffee was waiting for me I would have ran the whole way," he joked to lighten the mood. It had the desired effect as Rachel and Carlos both laughed. "Besides, it was probably better to come this way. It was nice to have someone to make the trip with. I'm sure it's going to be lonely trying to make it to Yucaipa by myself. Plus, I got to sleep in a real bed and not under the stars. Or under the aurora I guess," Rob added.

"Well I'm glad you decided to as well," Rachel said. "That was a crazy night."

"Yes, it was," Rob said quietly as he thought about everything they experienced the night before, then changed the conversation. "Hey, I don't want to impose or sound like a know-it-all or sound like I'm talking down to you guys, so just tell me if you don't want my advice and I'll shut up, but I've thought about a scenario like what's going on for a long time and I have some ideas about how to make your situation here a little safer and more sustainable. I'm more than happy to tell you guys what I think about your setup here and give you some tips if you want me to."

"Yeah man I would appreciate that," Carlos said. "I've thought about protecting my family, but more for a 'bump in the night' type situation, not like what we have going on now. Rachel also told me about the hospital. Unbelievable," Carlos was shaking his head.

"And it's going to get worse, I can just about guarantee that. It's only a matter of time before some mob or gang comes here looking for stuff. Especially since this is one of the nicer neighborhoods on this side of the city. Everyone that has nothing will think all the nicer areas have what they need and will start looting them after the stores are all empty," Rob said while shaking his head. "My plan is to leave around sunset so that gives us a couple hours to go over stuff. Give me a minute and let me grab something to eat from my backpack and we'll get started," Rob replied.

"No need for that Rob," Rachel interrupted. "Here you go." She handed him a plate full of cheese, crackers and slices of salami."

"Are you sure?" Rob asked. "I don't want to cut into your food supplies here. You might need to ration it and I can eat what I have in my bag."

"It's the least we can do," Rachel replied. "Eat up and I'll refill your coffee."

"Thanks guys," Rob said as he sat at the large wood dinner table. "We can actually get started while I eat. I'm sure you both know the standard stuff of power outages, don't open the refrigerator unless you have to, keep the candles handy, stuff like that?" They both nodded in the affirmative as Rob kept putting food into his mouth. He knew it was rude, and his wife wouldn't approve, but he talked between bites. He had bigger fish to fry than worry about his manners and he was sure Carlos and Rachel wouldn't care, especially as he was going over stuff that might help them survive.

"This situation is pretty similar," Rob continued. "The difference being nothing electronic works of course, and the power outage isn't going to last just a few hours or days. It's going to go on for a long time, probably for years. So, one of the most important things is for you guys to think with a more long-term mindset in terms of food and water, and a security mindset in terms of your house and neighborhood here. The good news is your house is set next to a storm drain and I noticed the large jacuzzi in the back when I went out there. You also have cinder block wall surrounding the entire backyard except for the little gate in the back that lets out to the wash area. The bad news is that it's the first house set off the main road, so security will be a little more difficult because your house could very well be the first targeted by anyone trying to score supplies for themselves. In terms of your food, you want to eat what's in the refrigerator first, then work on the freezer second, before you really get into anything that's in your pantry. With any canned goods you have…"

"We have quite a bit. I do some couponing on my days off," Rachel interjected.

Rob nodded and continued, "… you want to save that for last. The canned food will be good for quite a while, even after the expiration date. Do you guys have any water stored?" Rob asked as he finished the food on the plate in front of him.

"I have about twenty cases of bottled water in the garage. I keep it on hand for my work crews during the summer. We also have nine or ten 5-gallon water jugs for the water dispenser on the wall next to you. Those are all full, I filled them a couple days ago," Carlos paused for a moment and Rob could see him thinking. "We also have the jacuzzi you mentioned. It's a large one, I think it holds something like 500 gallons. I just refilled it too because the weather was finally warming up enough to enjoy it again. I think that's all we have."

"That's pretty good. That's more than most of your neighbors are going to have. Do you guys still have water pressure in the lines?"

Rachel reached over and quickly pushed up then back down on the kitchen sink faucet handle. The water came out at less than half its normal pressure.

"Okay, first things first," Rob said with urgency in his voice. "As fast as you guys can get any containers you have. Even your trash can, put a new bag in it and use it. Plastic storage bins, empty water bottles, anything, and start filling them up. That pressure isn't going to last long. Even your bath tubs. Use your stoppers and fill them up. Hurry!"

Both Carlos and Rachel sprang into action. Carlos took the trash can, pulled the half full bag and put it next to the back door, got a new bag and put it inside, then put the can on the floor in front of the sink. Their sink had a pull-out faucet that could be used like a hose, so he pulled it out all the way and turned on the water. Rob walked over, "Let me hold this. Get out your bowls and storage containers."

Rachel was already in the guest bathroom in the hallway. She quickly plugged the drain with the rubber stopper and turned the water on all the way then moved upstairs to the master bath and did the same. The third bathroom, the one attached to the room Rob had slept in, only had a walk-in shower stall, no tub. On her way out of the master bath she picked up the small trash can from the bathroom and took it downstairs. On her way past the guest bathroom she grabbed the small trash can out of there as well. She came into the kitchen, took the used bags out of the small cans, and set the cans on the counter next to the sink. "I think we are out of bags for these ones."

"That's fine," Rob said. "Still use them. The water can be used for a lot of things even if you can't drink it." By this time the large trash can was almost full, so he started filling the plastic storage containers Carlos had pulled from the cupboards. Rachel went back to the bathrooms to check the status of the tubs and while Carlos disappeared into the backyard.

Rob finished filling the storage containers and small trash cans then turned off the water. While he was thinking of anything else they could use to store water Carlos came walking in from the back yard. "I have a large forty-five-gallon trash can I use for my yard work. I put a new bag in it and started filling it using the hose out there."

"Good thinking," replied Rob. "Between the tubs and everything here, and that trashcan out there, you guys might get another one or two hundred gallons."

Rachel came back into the kitchen. "Both tubs are full and there is still a little bit of pressure in the lines. Not much but it's there."

"With any luck it will hold and fill up the trashcan out back," Carlos said before he walked back out to check the trash can.

Rob followed him out and checked the can. It was about half full and the water from the hose had slowed to almost nothing. "Just let it keep going. Every little bit will help in the long run."

It was another five minutes before the water pressure completely gave out, leaving the trash can about three quarters full. "Let's head back inside and go over things with Rachel," Rob said as he walked back towards the house.

Before he reached the backdoor Carlos stopped him, "Hey hold up, do you hear that?"

Rob stopped and listened, but all was quiet. "What's up?" He asked as he started looking around the backyard, checking to make sure whatever Carlos was hearing wasn't someone trying prowl around the house. He noticed Carlos looking into the sky, searching back and forth. *What the heck is he doing?*

Carlos walked to the back wooden gate in the middle of the block wall and looked over and to the east, still looking into the sky. Finally, Rob heard it. It was faint, but unmistakably the *whoop-whoop-whoop* sound of a helicopter. Rob started searching the sky as well. It was another minute, with the sound growing louder and louder, before the helicopter suddenly appeared from behind the hills that were at the eastern end of the neighborhood. It was flying in a westerly direction and moving fast.

"That's a Blackhawk. Army I think," Carlos commented. Rob didn't know much about military aircraft but knew what a Blackhawk looked like from his younger days playing video games and watching military movies. "Probably going to

March," Carlos continued. "Wonder how the chopper still works when nothing else does. The Army typically doesn't have stuff hardened against EMP's."

Rachel suddenly burst out of the backdoor of the house. "Was that a helicopter I heard?"

"Yeah, Blackhawk heading west," Carlos confirmed. At this point the helicopter was out of view but was still faintly audible.

"I thought nothing worked though? Helicopters have computers and electronics. How is it flying?" Rachel asked, confusion in her voice.

"I don't know," Carlos answered. "I was just telling Rob the same thing; the Army doesn't typically have stuff hardened against EMP's. I have no clue. At least the military might still be functioning a little. That's good news."

Once the sound of the chopper completely faded away, and after another minute of all three looking into the sky hoping to spot another one, Rob interrupted the silence. "Let's head inside and go over some more stuff," he said.

They walked back into the kitchen where Rachel quickly cleaned up Rob's lunch plate and empty coffee cup then joined Rob and Carlos at the dinner table.

Rob began, "If your tubs are standard size they probably hold around eighty gallons each. By my estimate you guys were able to get another two hundred or more gallons of water before the water pressure ran out. Besides the five hundred or so gallons in the hot tub, you guys also have the water tanks on the backs of the toilets and the hot water heater you can get water from. To make the water safe to drink, you need to bring it to a boil before drinking it. You don't need to let it boil for a long time or anything, just bring it to a rolling boil then let it cool. That will kill any bacteria in the water. If you guys are unable to boil it, you can use bleach as long as its regular unscented bleach. It takes about eight drops per gallon of water. Put in the bleach, give the water a little stir, then wait for thirty minutes to an hour for it to be drinkable. If you taste a little bit of chlorine, it's okay to drink. The other thing with water, no amount of boiling or bleach will remove chemicals. That's good for germs only. You can use charcoal to help you filter out some chemicals but if you aren't sure I would just use any water with chemicals for hygiene purposes and use your clean water to drink and cook food. You might want to think of a way to capture rain water as well since it's almost April and there might be a few more storms before summer really arrives."

Rob paused for a minute when Rachel pulled out a notebook and a pen from a drawer. He smiled as she made notes of the information he was relaying. *She's taking it seriously. They might have a chance.* Once she was finished writing Rob asked, "You both ready to talk security?"

"Yeah," they both said at the same time. "Samantha just went down for her nap, so we have a little time," Rachel continued.

"You guys have any weapons?" Rob asked. Carlos stood up and waved for Rob to follow. He led Rob out to the garage, with Rachel following, and up to a good size safe.

Carlos tried to punch in the code on the electronic keypad but got no response. "Ah hell, the EMP killed the keypad too. Damn! Good thing I have a backup key." Carlos walked over to the washer and dryer next to the door that led into the house. He reached around the back of the washer and pulled off a key he had taped to the back when he first had the safe installed. He came back over to the safe, removed the round keypad by turning the entire electronic assembly counter clockwise and pulling out, then inserted the key into a slot behind the keypad and turned. Rob heard a click and watched as Carlos turned the handle on the front door to release the security pins holding the door closed. When the door opened Rob looked inside and was impressed with what he saw. Just from his initial look he could see two AR-15 rifles, a Mini-14 rifle, three shotguns, and several handguns in holders on the inside panel of the door. On the bottom left side of the safe were several ammo cans that he assumed stored ammo.

"Dude you got some fire power," Rob said. "And I see your AR's aren't the neutered 'California-Compliant' bullshit models."

Carlos responded, "They do have bullet buttons, but I have regular mag releases that I can swap out. Takes about five minutes. I grew up in Texas, my whole family hunts and shoots regularly. I settled down here after getting out of the Army. Served for six years."

"A soldier?" Rob laughed. "You should be teaching me about security, not the other way around."

Carlos laughed with Rob, "Yeah, but I've never thought about having to fortify my own house before and you said you have thought about it, so I figured you could show me a few things. And besides, I wasn't infantry, I was a communications specialist assigned to a headquarters unit. Even during my two tours in Afghanistan I never saw any combat."

"That's how you knew about the chopper," Rob said as Carlos nodded. "Well I'll do my best, but no promises. First, I suggest you both start wearing sidearms at all times and keep one of the long guns nearby, but that of course is up to you. Rachel saw first-hand what's going on out there, and that's just the beginning. If you guys have any reservations about using these guns to protect yourselves you need to get it into your head, and fast, that you might have to pull the trigger first and ask questions later. This situation is going downhill and downhill fast, and it's going to be awhile before it starts going back the other way. There's no help coming now, no cops rolling code three to your 9-1-1 call, no firefighters coming to put out your house fire, no paramedics coming to swoop you up and take you to the nearest trauma center." Carlos was nodding and had a sober look on his face.

"Second, there is safety in numbers as the old saying goes. If you guys know your neighbors, you might want to set up a neighborhood watch type program and set up twenty-four-hour patrols that can watch the street. You can use some of the cars that no longer run to set up a roadblock where your street meets Moreno Beach. And think about setting up an early warning system of some sort. If you can get your neighbors to participate in manning the roadblock, whoever is there can sound a warning of some sort and let the neighborhood know something is going on. Could be something simple like a large drum or loud bell or airhorn or something. Carlos, you have any construction supplies?"

"Yeah I'll show you. But first, let me do this," Carlos said as he pulled a Sig Sauer handgun from a holder on the door. Once he loaded two magazines and found a holster for the gun he said, "That's better. Rachel we'll get you set up once Rob is all done."

"Good idea. After last night there is no good reason we should be walking around without protection from now on," Rachel said as she closed the safe door.

"All the construction supplies are in that trailer on the side of the house. I use it for work to run stuff back and forth to job sites when I'm not helping my team bid new jobs," Carlos explained as he walked back into the house then out the front door and over to the driveway. He took out a set of keys and used one to open the padlock that secured the doors on the back of the twenty-foot enclosed trailer. When he opened it, Rob could see the trailer was full of all kinds of things related to construction, from lumber and pipes to power tools and buckets of nails.

"Carlos," Rob said. "With your construction and Army background, you guys are going to be okay, especially with these supplies. What you need to do is take both of those skill sets and try to apply it to your house and neighborhood security. Even though you never saw combat you had to have some tactical training, even way back in basic."

Rob turned to face the house and started pointing out different features as he talked. "Personally, I would board up the windows on the first floor. And not with plywood, I'm thinking something heavier that might help stop or at least slow down shots being fired that direction. On the second floor I'd set up some shooting positions in those windows facing the street and especially in that one facing west towards Moreno Beach. Most likely that's where anyone with bad intentions are going to come from. If you have enough supplies, set up a position in one of the windows overlooking the golf course. Most likely a mob wouldn't come from the course but it's a good spot to keep a watch on the area to the north. Use some of the four by four pieces of lumber to reinforce the walls around the windows you are going to use to shoot from. You know as well as I do that these walls aren't going to stop much. With the wood it should give you some cover, especially if you double it up."

Rob now turned and looked at the neighbors houses, "And it looks like most of your neighbor's houses are two stories. If any of them have rifles and can shoot, then they can set up shooting positions same as you. If you get enough people involved, you guys could create a serious killing zone on the streets and I doubt any group would have much of a chance to take over." Rob could see Rachel writing furiously in the notebook, so he paused a moment to let her catch up.

When she stopped writing he continued, "Also, if you can, besides the roadblock, you can take some cars and position them to create choke points out on Moreno Beach. Make sure the choke points are positioned so that they can be easily seen from the second story windows, then it would be even easier to repel an attack by large groups. In the long run you might even think about building some boxes and filling them with dirt or sand. You can put them in the street, even building it all the way across. If you build a box that is two feet thick and fill it up, that will pretty much stop anything that is fired your way. And that reminds me, when you are using cars for cover, make sure you are behind the engine block if possible, or at least behind the wheels. Even small rounds will go right through the doors and side panels, so the cars aren't the best use for cover. Let's head to the backyard."

All three walked into the backyard where Rob pointed to the rear cinder block wall. "Carlos you should be able to set something up for when nature calls. If it were me I'd dig a large hole somewhere on the other side of the wall and down the slope well away from the house, then use some of that four-inch PVC pipe I seen in the trailer to fashion a sewer type system. You can cover the hole with plywood and throw some dirt on top to help keep it in place. The only problem is using water to help flush it down the pipe, but you might be able to come up with something that will let you do it. You can set up an outhouse back here and use the slope to your advantage."

"That's a great idea. I never thought of that," Carlos said as he looked around the backyard with a thoughtful look on his face.

"Also, trash is going to be an issue. The trash truck isn't going to be coming around once a week anymore of course so you guys will have to dispose of any trash you create. You should try to recycle anything you are able to instead of just tossing it. Anything you can't recycle into some other use I would burn, maybe in a sand trap on the golf course or one of the fields nearby."

"Looks like I'm going to have my work cut out for me," Carlos said with a determined look on his face.

"Looks that way," Rob agreed as he looked at his watch. 5:48 pm. He looked to the west and could see the sun was starting to get low in the sky. "Carlos, before I head out do you mind if I use your cleaning kit to clean my gun?"

"No man, not at all, lets head to the garage and I'll get you set up," Carlos said as he turned and waved for Rob to follow.

Rob followed Carlos to a work bench that was set up next to the safe in the garage. Carlos showed Rob where he stored his cleaning supplies and Rob got to work. He released the magazine and set it aside then pulled back the slide and released the round from the chamber. He field-stripped the gun and quickly cleaned the barrel, slide, and lower receiver. He had only fired one round through it so there was almost no need to clean it, but Rob wanted to be as prepared as possible.

Once he was done he reassembled the gun, slammed the magazine home in the grip, and pulled back the slide then released it to chamber a round. Then he released the magazine again, put the loose round into it, and placed the magazine back into the gun. Now he had seventeen rounds ready to go, sixteen in the magazine and one in the chamber.

Rob walked back to the kitchen where he found Carlos and Rachel at the table, "Well guys, if you don't have any other questions for me I'm going to start gathering my stuff. It's about that time."

"You sure you don't want to stay another day? The rest might do you good," Rachel offered.

"No, thank you for offering though. I need to keep moving. It's still a long way home, and unless my brother made it to my house, my wife and son are there alone. I know she can handle things on her own, and we have good neighbors, but I'm still going to worry until I'm home." Being a cop, Rob's brother Matt had attended similar terrorism training classes and received much the same information that Rob did. Together they planned out what to do if an EMP ever occurred and decided it made most sense for Matt to make his way to Rob's house. Rob didn't know if Matt was working when the EMP hit, but Rob knew wherever he was he would be headed to Rob's house as well. Rob just hoped his brother was a lot closer than Rob was. The only thing that would delay Matt was if he stopped at his apartment to gather his own weapons and ammo on the way to Rob's house.

"I understand Rob, I'd do the same thing," Carlos replied. Rob went upstairs and into the guest bedroom. He made the bed then packed his dirty clothes into his backpack and carried it back downstairs just as Carlos was walking back into the kitchen from the garage. He was holding an older Marlin .22 Long Rifle caliber bolt action rifle and a small box of ammunition.

"Hey Rob, nothing I do or say can ever express my thanks for keeping Rachel safe and making sure she got back home to me. I owe you everything for that. All the other stuff you helped us with, including the water, is just the cherry on top. Rachel said you're trying to walk to Yucaipa, that's quite a hike, and you're going to need a little bit more than that nine you're carrying on your hip. This is for you," he handed the rifle to Rob. "It's not much but I'm sure it'll help you on the way home."

"Are you sure man? This gun is worth its weight in gold in this new world of ours," Rob was dumbfounded that Carlos would part with it. The little rifle was perfect for hunting small game and used properly could be used at ranges out to a couple hundred yards. It probably wouldn't kill a human unless Rob hit them in the head with the bullet, but no one wanted to be shot so he was confident it would be useful even against two-legged predators.

"I'm positive. Like I said, you saved Rachel's life. That's priceless to me," Carlos said quietly and with sincerity. "It shoots straight. I've had it since I was twelve. It was one of my birthday gifts."

"Wow. Thanks man, this will definitely help me get home."

Rob released the ten-round magazine. It was full. He pulled the bolt back and found the chamber empty. He took a moment to fashion a two-point sling out of the paracord from his backpack. Then he used a little more paracord and a carabiner from a small pouch on the backpack to make a quick release attachment so that he could secure the gun vertically on the right side of his backpack with the barrel pointed down. This way it would be out of the way if he needed to run or fight but would still be quickly accessible if he needed to use it. If he reached back over his shoulder he could grab the stock, and if he pulled straight up he was able to get the gun free of the paracord and bring the gun around without taking off his backpack. It wouldn't be fast getting it out of the makeshift paracord holster and he would never be able to re-attach it without taking off the backpack, but Rob didn't mind. Having a small rifle would be invaluable on the trek home.

"You're welcome Rob, I wish there was more I could do for you," he handed the box of ammo to Rob then pulled two more ten-round magazines from his pocket. Both full, Rob could see as he took them from Carlos. That gave him a total eighty rounds of .22 Long Rifle.

"There is one thing. You mind if I fill up on water?"

"Shoot, why didn't I think of that?" the rhetorical question came from Rachel, who jumped up from the table and took the canteen and water pouch from Rob once he freed them from his backpack. "Give me your empty water bottle too, the one in your bag." Rob handed it over and Rachel used one of the plastic storage containers to fill up all three. Once they were full she handed them both back and Rob stowed them in their places.

"Well guys, I guess this is it," Rob said.

Carlos came over and gave Rob a bear hug, "Thanks again buddy. I'll say a prayer for your family. Get home safe to them. Good luck out there."

"No problem man, good luck to you guys too. Thanks for letting me rest up." Rob started to feel a little emotional knowing there was a very good chance he would never see them again. There was an unspoken bond between him and Rachel now, the kind that only comes from facing death together, and Carlos was a great guy who under different circumstance Rob was sure would be a good friend.

Next Rachel threw her arms around him. "Thank you so, so much. I don't think I would have made it home if you hadn't walked here with me. I hope one day we see each other again. Get home and take care of your family. Be safe out there," she said, her voice cracking.

"Thanks for keeping me company on the way here. Maybe one day when this is all over we'll get together and trade war stories," he laughed. "Take care of the big guy alright?"

Next Rob got down on one knee and held his arms out to Samantha. "Do I get a hug?" She ran up to him and gave him a hug. "Take care of Momma and Papa okay? They need you to look after them, so they don't get into trouble." Samantha just giggled.

Rob stood, put his black Carhart jacket on, picked up the Eberlestock backpack again, and looked at his watch. 6:38 pm. "I'm going to head out the back way and cut through the golf course if you don't mind." He followed Carlos out and waited for him to unlock the back gate. Once he stepped through he started walking in a northeast direction along the drainage ditch. He turned around and could see Rachel and Carlos standing side by side, arms around each other, Samantha in front of them. All three waved at him as they smiled, with Rachel wiping a tear away from her cheek. He gave them one last wave before turning around and heading out.

CHAPTER 6

Rob walked east along the drainage ditch until it let out onto the golf course. His plan was to reach Redlands Boulevard and take it north for several miles to San Timoteo Canyon. Having golfed this very course in the past, Rob knew he could use the course to make it most of the way to Redlands and from Rachel's house it was about a mile east as the crow flew. Rob continued through the golf course, through the rapidly growing grass, over the fairways and greens, crossing several cart paths, and avoiding the roughs and sand-traps, using the trees for cover when he was able too, but otherwise just walking quickly through and watching his surroundings.

At one point an elderly lady yelled at him from the backyard of her house which faced the golf course.

"Hey, you're trespassing! Get off my golf course!" She yelled with a shrill voice.

"Your golf course? I didn't realize you owned it," Rob yelled back, voice dripping with sarcasm. "I thought it was open to the public."

The old lady, Rob thought she was in her seventies, sputtered for a minute while trying to come up with an answer, then finally said, "You're lucky there's something wrong with my phone or I'd already be calling the authorities. Just get the hell off the course young man!"

"Yes ma'am, right away ma'am," Rob threw a sarcastic salute in the direction of the house as he laughed. *Someone is having a bad day.*

"Lois! What're you doing? Leave that man alone!" Rob heard an elderly, but still loud, male voice from inside the house. "He's not doing anything."

"He's not supposed to be here!" the lady, Lois, yelled back into the house.

"Just get inside woman! If the TV was working you would've never noticed him in the first place," the male voice yelled back at Lois.

Rob laughed hard for a couple minutes before getting himself under control. *That's probably me and Monica in about forty years.*

As he walked, Rob reflected on the little bit of time he spent with Carlos and Rachel. He was glad he made the journey with Rachel to her house. They were good people and they had a better chance than most of surviving the coming chaos, especially with Carlos' military and construction background. It made Rob feel good that he was able help them out especially since they had a young daughter. Of course, the day of rest did him some good too.

He walked to the east end of the course and was able to cut north, walking through a gap in the houses where yet another drainage ditch was located. When he reached Cactus Avenue he was blocked by a six-foot high rod iron fence. There was a pedestrian gate, but it was secured with a padlock.

Before throwing his Eberlestock backpack over Rob took a good look around. On the other side of the street was a large open field, and Rob didn't see anyone or anything moving around in the area. From his vantage point he could see the sun would soon be below the horizon, so he removed the Surefire flashlight from his backpack and clipped the nylon holster to his belt just behind the Gerber knife. Since he did not want to drop the backpack over the fence for fear of damaging the Marlin rifle, he pulled some paracord out and tied it to the carry handle at the top of the pack. Holding onto the paracord, he tossed the backpack over then slowly lowered it to the ground. As he jumped the gate himself, he paused at the top to use the height to his advantage and take another quick look around to make sure he hadn't missed anything important.

He could see that the drainage ditch continued under the street and through the field north of Cactus. Next to the ditch was a dirt service road that angled to the northeast, the same direction Rob was going, so he decided to follow the dirt road instead of staying on Cactus Ave. After jumping down from the fence, he decided to leave the paracord in place on the backpack in case he needed to utilize the same technique in the future. He measured out about twenty feet of paracord then used the folding Gerber knife to cut off the rest, which he stowed in the backpack. The paracord still attached to the backpack he rolled up and tied onto the carry handle, so it was out of the way but still easily accessible.

He looked both directions one more time then crossed the street. There was a guardrail and fence that blocked his access, but they only continued for about a hundred feet, so he walked around the fence and into the field, moved onto the dirt road, and continued walking. The dirt road went for about a quarter mile before letting out onto Redlands.

Rob now had a decision to make. The spot where the dirt road intersected with Redlands was just south of an older neighborhood which stretched for about half a mile to the north. Rob could stay on the street and go straight through, or he could swing around to the east and walk through the massive open fields and farmland behind the neighborhood. The safest route was through the fields but that would potentially add hours to the trip. There was also an indoor farmer's market and small gas station on the road straight through.

Rob elected to go through the neighborhood mainly because of the market and gas station. He wanted to see if he could scavenge any food and knew that if anything happened and he needed to escape he could head east for one block and be into the fields. The other thing that influenced his decision was the sun was already below the horizon and darkness was starting to set in. He wanted to get through as fast as possible and the darkness would provide some cover, even in the twilight created by the aurora. There wasn't much natural or manmade cover in the way of trees or cars, so Rob walked at a fast clip and stayed next to the right side of the road, figuring he could jump a fence into someone's yard or just run east down one of the side streets if the need arose.

Rob got back into the habit of stopping at each cross street and checking both directions for movement before proceeding through the intersections. He went three blocks before arriving at the farmer's market which sat on the east side of Redlands in between the cross streets of Kimberly Avenue and Alessandro. Rob first checked both directions down the cross street, then turned his attention to the store and could see the front windows and glass front door were smashed out. *Someone beat me to it. It hasn't even been a full twenty-four hours since the incident, and stores are already being looted. Damn. Oh well, still worth a check, there might be stuff inside.*

Rob crossed Kimberly and walked into the parking lot of the store, then to the front right corner of the building, where he drew his gun. *Have to be ready for anything.* He looked through the smashed windows as he made his way along the front of the building, searching the interior for potential threats before entering the building, then stopped next to the front door to listen for any movement from inside. Hearing only silence he walked through the broken doorway, leading with his gun up and ready. After entering he immediately sidestepped left to get out of the "fatal funnel" as he scanned the interior of the building. There was trash and debris everywhere. *This wasn't the work of one person, this was an entire mob that came in and destroyed this place.* A series of fruit and vegetable displays divided the store into three aisles and the displays created numerous blind spots he needed to clear.

Before clearing the building, he dropped his backpack by the front door so he wouldn't be encumbered by his heavy pack if something happened. Ideally, he would have stashed it outside as it would be easier to come back and retrieve if he had to run from the building, but it would be disastrous if someone stole it while Rob was inside scavenging for supplies.

He cleared the store, activating the weapon mounted light only sporadically and using the brief moments of light to make a mental picture of the areas too dark to see. *I wish I had a partner, clearing a building by yourself sucks.* He checked behind each fruit and vegetable display and found nothing but more trash and debris. Next, he moved to the back and walked through the open door that led to the employee and storage area, checking down each row of metal shelves used to store product. Empty as well. He checked the door that led out back and found it was metal and had a dead bolt that required a key to open it from either side. *I don't think that complies to fire code. Not that it really matters anymore.*

Once the entire building was clear he holstered his gun and pulled out the Surefire flashlight as he walked to the storage shelves. There he found a box of plastic grocery bags and pulled one out, then walked back to the front customer area to check for anything he could scavenge.

All the junk food on the rack next to the checkout counter was gone, as were the sodas and bottled water from the cooler next to the door. Someone even took the time and effort to shatter the glass door of the cooler then rip the door from the hinges. *Senseless destruction. What the hell's the point?* Rob thought. Most of the fruit and vegetables were gone as well, however, there was enough scattered about, on top of the displays and on the floor, that Rob was able to scavenge four apples, three bananas, a small bunch of grapes, and three tomatoes. *All in all, a pretty good haul. It's more than I expected when I saw the store had already been looted. This will help a lot.* He retrieved his backpack and stuffed the grocery bag containing fruit into the large main compartment, on top of all the supplies. He was hungry but decided to get clear of the residential area before finding somewhere to eat and rest.

Before leaving the store, Rob peered out the front windows, checking the surrounding areas for a few minutes before deciding it was safe to go. He preferred to go out the locked back door, but it would take too much time and energy to get through the metal door and frame. He shouldered his backpack and left the building, making an immediate right and walking to the north side of the store and through the parking lot to Alessandro, which crossed between the farmer's market and the mom and pop gas station. It was the same Alessandro that ran in front of the dispatch center in Riverside, however here it was much narrower, one lane in each direction and divided by a yellow line.

He approached the street, scanning his surroundings the entire way, then crossed and walked up to the south side of the gas station building. The gas station was small, having two pumps out front, a small parking lot with seven parking spaces, and a propane fill station. Rob poked his head around to the front side of the building that faced west and could see the glass in the front door was shattered. He didn't really need anything from inside and he almost bypassed the gas station altogether, but he wanted to check for any water that was possibly still inside, left behind by the looters.

Once again Rob drew his gun and approached the front door slowly. This building's front windows were completely covered with advertisements showing what kinds of deals customers could expect inside, so Rob had no ability to check inside until he reached the front door.

He reached the broken glass door and listened. After hearing nothing he stepped quickly through the door and side stepped to the left while moving the gun left and right, his eyes following, checking every open area he possibly could. This building was much smaller than the farmer's market and the only areas he could not see was behind the cashier's counter, and of course the employee area in the back of the store. He took a quick look over the counter and confirmed no one was hiding there, put his backpack on top of the counter, then proceeded to the closed door that separated the public area from the employee area. After listening, he quickly opened the door and swept inside, the door squeaking as he pushed it open. He used his weapon mounted light to flood the open area and realized right away that it was occupied by three homeless people who had set up residence. All three were asleep and between the door squeaking open and the light from Rob's TLR-1 suddenly brightening the room, all three stirred.

Rob started to back away but the only female in the group was already sitting up and talking to him, "Who're you? Get that damn light outta my eyes!"

After quickly confirming there were no obvious weapons around the three Rob pointed his gun towards the ground in front of the trio. "Sorry, I didn't realize anyone was in here," he apologized.

One of the two males was now fully coherent and yelled at Rob, "Well there is! And you coulda knocked! You make it a habit of just walking into someone's house?"

"Your house? This is a gas station," Rob stated, puzzled.

"Not anymore," the female retorted, somewhat proud. "Ain't no way to pump gas, so we took over. It's our place now."

"Okay, sorry," Rob apologized again, trying to keep the situation from escalating. "I was just hoping to find a little water is all."

The third transient was still asleep. The male that was awake started to get up, "All this shit is ours, don't you be tryin to take any of it. I swear to God I'll cut you if you try."

Rob pointed his gun at the transient who was now on his feet. "Sit down or I'll shoot your ass," he said with command in his voice.

The transient hesitated, decided Rob was serious, then slowly sat down. "Hey man there's no need for any of that," he said with a conciliatory tone.

"You're right, there isn't," Rob replied sharply. "Just stay where you are, and I'll see myself out. You might want to wait a few minutes before checking to see if I'm gone too. If I think any of you are following me, I'll shoot first and ask questions later." Rob backed out of the employee area, picked up his backpack from the counter, and walked towards the front door.

As he walked he took a quick look around and at the end of the front aisle found several gallon size plastic water bottles. Rob picked one up and walked out. He didn't want to take the time to make sure the area was still clear, so he scanned as he walked. He walked straight out of the parking lot and turned right when he reached the street.

He started walking at a fast pace north on Redlands. Darkness had completely taken over the daylight at this point and while the aurora was back, it was not as strong as the night before. The light it created was less than a full moon, but still enough that Rob didn't need to use his flashlight to watch for potential hazards. In short order he crossed Williams, Gifford, and Stevens Avenues. When he reached the intersection of Redlands and Bay Avenue, the houses on the left continued to the north however on the right the houses stopped and opened into a huge field. As he stopped at the intersection to check both directions he started to hear a commotion from the east. He crouched and creeped forward, trying to get a visual of what was happening.

On the east side of Redlands, next to where Rob was at, a ditch ran north and south, paralleling the street and had a metal three feet diameter tunnel running under each cross street which allowed rain runoff to pass through without flooding the intersection. Rob hopped down into the ditch and moved closer to the intersection. That's when he could see it. A large group of people, around fifty Rob estimated, several holding flashlights and a few holding lanterns, but all of them holding various weapons. Most of the weapons being wielded were things like bats and poles and even shovels, but several were carrying guns. Rob picked out at least three long guns and two handguns. He was sure there were more, but his view was blocked by the front of the crowd.

Rob had to think fast. The crowd was less than seventy-five feet away and approaching fast. There was no way he could make it to the previous cross street and make the turn without at least one of the group spotting him and he knew he couldn't run, no one can outrun a bullet, so the only option was to hide and hope for the best. There were no parked cars close enough, and the house he was next to had no cover in the front yard. His only option was the tunnel. He pushed his backpack and gallon of water into the tunnel then went in feet first, pushing the pack and water along until he was about five feet into the tunnel, where he stopped and drew his gun. There was no way he could shoot every member of the group, and if it came to that almost certainly he would be a dead man, but he wouldn't go down without a fight. And it was possible the first few going down after being shot would cause the rest to scatter and give Rob a chance to escape.

As Rob waited and prayed that no one would investigate the

tunnel, he heard the crowd approach the intersection. They were obviously worked up about something, but what it was Rob didn't know. The crowd stopped when they arrived at the intersection and quieted down some and Rob could hear one person addressing the rest of the group. He couldn't make out what was being said, but it was obvious the leader was giving instructions to the rest of the group.

Another two minutes passed before the crowd got loud again and moved off. Unfortunately for Rob, they split into two roughly even sized groups with one going south on Redlands, the other west on Bay. *Damnit, now I have two groups to contend with.* The only good news was that Rob was headed north, away from both groups. The bad news was he needed to figure out how to get out of the tunnel and make it north of the intersection without being spotted. Rob wasn't sure what the groups were up to and he couldn't risk that they were watching the area for anyone passing through. *A group like that, all worked up and ready to cause havoc, wouldn't hesitate a second to beat me to a pulp, if not kill me, and take my stuff.*

Rob turned as much as he could and looked down the length of the tunnel. Blackness. He holstered his gun, pulled out his flashlight, and covering the light with is hand to reduce the chance of someone seeing the beam of light, he turned it on, then slowly separated his fingers to allow some of the light to seep through. About halfway down the pipe there was some debris blocking half the tunnel. Rob decided it was worth a try and with only a little difficulty got turned around. He started army crawling forward, pushing his backpack and gallon of water in front of him, until he reached the debris pile. Using the flashlight, he could now see that it was a combination of trash and tree branches. The good news was that there wasn't very much of it.

Rob went to work quietly moving enough of the debris out of the way to create a large enough opening to crawl through. It took about five minutes, but he was soon on his way. Once he reached the north end of the tunnel, on the side of Bay that he needed to be on, he paused and listened. While trying to make sure the groups were no longer in the area he dug into his backpack and took his beanie out. It wasn't very cold, but the black beanie would be much less likely to catch someone's eye in the darkness than his bald white head. He also took out a pair of black gloves and put them on. The darker his profile, the better.

When he was ready he pushed the backpack and water slowly out of the tunnel and followed it, getting into a low crouch and slowly looking around the intersection and as far down each street as he could, trying to see any evidence of either group. He could hear some yelling, but it seemed to be at least a few blocks away. Once he was reasonably certain that it was safe to move he shouldered his backpack, picked up his gallon of water, and took off, still in a crouch but moving as fast as he could. He decided to stay in the ditch as long as possible to reduce his chances of being seen.

Less than a quarter mile later Redlands widened out from a single lane in each direction divided by a yellow line, to a single lane in each direction but now divided by a large landscaped island with a large shoulder on the west side of the street. This was due to a new housing development that was built in the last couple years. The thing that appealed to Rob was the horse trail that was set between the sidewalk and the block wall that separated the backyards of the houses from the main street. The horse trail was also partially hidden by bushes and would offer some cover, however Rob had to cross the street to get to it.

He took a good look back to the south and waited. Nothing. He crawled out of the ditch and to the edge of the street. Still nothing. He decided to it was time and took off at a run. He was across in a few seconds and hunkered down behind a bush. He watched for a couple more minutes until he was satisfied that the mob didn't see him cross the street and wasn't coming north to investigate.

Rob took a couple large drinks of water from the gallon he was carrying then opened his Eberlestock backpack and partially pulled out the water pouch. Using the plastic gallon, he topped off the water pouch then pushed the pouch back in. There was about half a gallon left. Rob took a couple more drinks then closed the container and set it aside. He had to pee. Not bothering to find a suitable place, he stood up, unzipped his pants, and relieved himself where he stood, preferring to keep a vigilant watch rather than worry about privacy. Once he was done he zipped back up, picked up the plastic water container, and walked north, using the horse trail.

Rob came to the intersection of Redlands and Cottonwood Avenue, did his usual check of the area, and proceeded across, walking back onto the horse trail as it continued heading north. He needed to rest but had yet to see somewhere he was comfortable doing so. Instead, he powered on. During one of his times walking backwards he noticed a glow in the sky. *That's not the aurora,* he thought. It was coming from the area of the gas station and farmer's market. The next time he turned around to check his rear he could see flames rising above the tree line. *Fire. I wonder if that group has anything to do with it. I'm glad I made it through when I did. Maybe that mob tried to loot the gas station and those transients fought back, with that being the result.* Rob shook his head as he turned to keep walking.

Rob crossed the intersection of Redlands and Dracaea Avenue. At this point Redlands narrowed back down; one lane each direction with a yellow line in the middle. While the horse trail also ended, so did the neighborhoods, and large fields stretched out on both sides of the street. He was happy to be out of the neighborhoods, but still did not want to stop until he found a place with suitable cover, so he pushed on. If he was going to rest, he didn't want to be out in the open where he could be seen. At the next intersection, Redlands and Eucalyptus Avenue, there was a large plant nursery. *That would be perfect. I doubt anyone is there, and I can hide on the property in the middle of the trees and plants while I rest.* What wasn't perfect was the tall chain link fence topped with razor wire that surrounded the property.

Rob walked until he came to the main entrance off Redlands. The gate here was just as tall but had no razor wire on top. Before climbing over Rob gave the gate a strong shake and let loose a low whistle. He wanted to make sure there were no dogs on the property. After a minute with no response he scaled the gate, not bothering to throw his backpack over first as the chain link made climbing easy and dropped down on the other side.

He walked into the property and found the main office where customers contacted employees and paid for any product they selected from the grounds. Rob tried the door and found it locked, so he continued to look around the property until he came across a stack of hay bales situated next to a large area of potted trees. *Bingo. That's going to make a nice spot to rest.* Rob finished walking through the rest of the property to be sure it was unoccupied, then walked back to the bales of hay. He reached up to one on top, and pulled, letting it fall to the ground, and repeated the action twice more, then pulled the machete out of the sheath on the backpack. He put the backpack on the ground to the side and went to work on the bales. They were bound together with three thick strings, but using the machete Rob was able to get the strings cut off without any trouble. He did the same for the other two bales, arranged the now loose hay into a pile, and then sat down.

He sighed with relief. *That's nice. If I didn't have to get home I'd stay here awhile.* Rob checked the time. 9:49 pm. Almost three hours since he left Carlos and Rachel's house. Three hours to cover two and a half miles. It might take him a little longer than he thought to make it home, especially if things were worse when he reached Yucaipa. He reached into his pocket and pulled the picture of his wife and son out, stared at it for a minute, said a quick prayer asking God to keep them safe until he got home, gave it a kiss, then put it back in his pocket.

Rob reached over and pulled the bag with his pilfered fruit out of the backpack. In all the action one of the bananas and a tomato was smashed but the rest seemed to be fine. He didn't care how smashed it was, it was still good to eat. He ate the smashed banana first, then the tomato, a few grapes, half a bag of nuts he still had from the first gas station he broke into, then started working on the half gallon of water he was still carrying.

As he relaxed he thought about what was going on. *Not quite twenty-four hours in. I've broken into a gas station. Fended off a dog using an ASP. Avoided the smoke from a plane crash. Shot and almost certainly killed someone. Watched as the hospital was over-run. Watched that random helicopter flying over. The farmer's market was looted and the transients set up residence in the gas station. I watched that mob move through the neighborhood. And if I had to bet that fire I saw was them setting fire to the gas station. That's more than most people see in a lifetime. What else will I witness before it's all over? What will my son witness as he grows up? The sad part is my son will grow up never knowing the life of excess and luxury that most Americans knew. Even those who were considered below the poverty line lived better than the vast majority of the world. My son won't get the joy of Saturday morning cartoons, the first day of school, going to the movies and mall with his friends, getting his license, girlfriends and all the issues that go with that. I hope Jackson and Monica are doing okay. I'm sure she's worrying about me as much as I'm worrying about them. Hopefully the neighbors were home when the EMP hit.*

Rob's street was a small one and all the neighbors knew and looked out for each other. They had occasional neighborhood bar-b-ques and if anyone went on vacation the other neighbors watched the house, got the mail, made sure the trashcans were put out if needed for trash day, made sure the pets were taken care of, all the things that made good neighbors. As his mind raced back and forth thinking about everything and nothing, his mood turned dark. After letting his mind wander for several minutes he thought to himself, *Enough of that. There will be enough time to cry over what I can't control. Right now, I have to focus on what I can control, which is getting home to my family.* Once again, he refocused his despair into determination.

Rob rested for thirty minutes before gathering his stuff. Before leaving his makeshift bed of hay he drank one of the 5-hour energy shots he was carrying then retraced his steps back to the main office and looked through the windows. When he didn't readily see anything that might help him on his trek home he moved on.

He reached the main gate and as he took a few minutes to study the surrounding area he thought he saw some movement in the field on the east side of the street. He ducked behind one of the large trees set next to the fence and continued to watch. Another minute passed before he was certain he could see something, but it wasn't until he heard barking that he realized it was several dogs walking in a southerly direction. He waited another five minutes to give them time to clear the area then climbed the gate and continued north. He walked on the left side of the road on the dirt shoulder and for the next half mile there was nothing around except fields.

As he walked, Rob admired the aurora and the quiet that seemed to blanket the earth. He wondered how the rest of the country was doing. His research always indicated that with a solar flare no country on earth would be spared, especially if the resulting EMP was similar in size, or even larger than, the Carrington Event of the 1800's. As he thought about it, Rob was sure the large cities like Los Angeles and New York in the United States, and cities like Moscow and Tokyo overseas, were descending into chaos. With limited resources and little to no law enforcement or military presence anywhere, the gangs would soon take over. They would seize what was left and rule their areas much like warlords and dictators in third world countries, using their power and ruthlessness to beat fear and submission into the population.

The rural areas and areas around military bases would fare much better, at least initially, until large groups of people made their way out of the city, seeking respite from the gangs or thinking there was a better chance at survival somewhere else. He wondered if he would come across anyone with a working radio that could at least receive any messages being broadcast by anyone that still had the capability.

Soon Rob was approaching State Highway 60, the initial route he planned to take home the night before. Redlands Boulevard remained narrow with one lane each direction divided by a yellow line and no sidewalks as it rose above the freeway and descended back down on the other side.

Several hundred feet short of the freeway Rob came to a stop and studied the area in front of him. He debated if he should stay on the road and cross the freeway using the overpass or walk down onto the freeway and cross the freeway itself. The pro to staying on Redlands was that it was a straight shot across and would give him good views of the area. The con was that once he was up on the bridge there was nowhere to go if he was surrounded by anyone that might be lying in wait to ambush unsuspecting travelers. The con to crossing the freeway itself was he would need to navigate the center divider and cross directly beneath the bridge created by the street, but the pro was he would have room to move if need be. He decided on the low route.

Rob proceeded north on Redlands, then turned left onto the eastbound onramp. The onramp made a sweeping U-turn and transitioned into the eastbound lanes before making its way under the overpass and continuing east. He walked onto the on ramp and followed the turn, the entire time scanning the overpass and freeway itself for anything that might appear out of place. He reached the freeway proper without incident and started to cross the eastbound lanes. When he reached the center divider he realized he only needed to get over the construction k-rails that were set up to protect freeway workers, instead of the usual concrete wall and vegetation that divided most of the freeway in this area. *That's right, now I remember. They have been working on expanding the freeway right here, prepping for future, and desperately needed, overpass and lane expansions. Guess that's never gonna happen now though.*

Rob easily hopped over the k-rail and passed over to the westbound lanes. He passed under the overpass, so he was now walking on the east side of the bridge and walked onto the westbound onramp which was a mirror image of the eastbound onramp. He walked up the onramp and followed it as it curved left and met back up with Redlands. When he was able to he looked south and studied the overpass, trying to see if there was anyone up there. He still couldn't see anyone but decided he'd rather be paranoid and alive, than lazy and captured or worse.

He turned north and started walking, this time on the left side of the street to put distance between himself and the few houses on the right. He was just past a group of five houses when he heard some screaming. He immediately scrambled down into the drainage ditch to his left, this one several feet deeper than the one used to hide from the group before, and slowly raised his head above the edge of the ditch, searching the area where the houses were. A few seconds later a male came out of the second house from the end, yelling something Rob couldn't make out and he was followed by a female who seemed to be yelling something back at the male. Rob watched for a few minutes as the two argued, screamed, and yelled at each other in the front yard of the house before they both walked back inside, the male punching the screen door and slamming the front door behind him. Rob shook his head. *Even during the end of the world people can't get along.* Once the couple was back inside the house Rob climbed out of the ditch and continued his trek north.

When Rob arrived at the intersection of Redlands and Iron-wood Avenue he didn't bother stopping to check in each direction as the open fields and flat land gave him a good field of view to check for trouble before he ever reached the intersection. As he continued north he entered a small community where the houses were generally larger and on bigger properties, many on two or more acres.

As he walked Rob never caught sight of a candle or heard anything other than the sounds of nature. He walked until he came to a very large church on the left side of the roadway. He decided to see if there was any running water and veered through the parking lot and up to the large building where he found a spigot on the front of the building and turned the handle, but nothing came out. *Oh well, it was worth a shot. Nature is calling anyways, this is as good a place as any.*

Rob walked around the backside of the church and found a large grass area with several trees and bushes. He selected one and used the Kershaw Siege to dig a hole. Once he was done he covered up the hole then refilled the water pouch using the last of the water from the one-gallon plastic bottle from the gas station, then flattened the bottle and put it into his backpack.

Rob walked back through the parking lot and linked back up with Redlands at the intersection of Kalmia Avenue. He knew soon he would have to tackle a steep incline that lasted for about a mile and was not looking forward to it. *Let's just get it done, its downhill for a few miles after that.* Rob set out again, passing houses on both sides, watching and hoping everyone was asleep so he could pass through unmolested. He soon passed the intersection with Locust Avenue and started the uphill climb. It was tough going but he set a steady pace and kept putting one foot in front of the other.

When he reached the crest, he stopped to catch his breath and turned to look at the city of Moreno Valley. He was shocked at the number of fires he could see. It seemed like every neighborhood had at least one house, and many two, that were burning. He could even see what looked like a large apartment building fully engulfed in flames. *That is insane.* Due to the light being cast onto the city from the aurora Rob could see several neighborhoods where it appeared entire blocks were burned down. With no ability for fire department response, fires burned unimpeded, only stopping when they ran out of fuel.

Rob said a quick prayer for the people affected by the carnage, and for his own family and friends, then turned and left Moreno Valley behind. The next part of his journey would be a whole different ball game and he was as determined as ever to make it home to his family.

CHAPTER 7

Rob checked the time. 12:32 am. With thoughts of how his family was doing, he started the descent into San Timoteo Canyon. Here, the street, one lane each direction with a double yellow solid line down the middle, was cut directly through the hill and had shear walls at least fifty feet high on both sides. As he rounded the first bend in the road Rob slowed. Stopped directly in the middle of the street facing him was a brand new black Chevy Tahoe. He made sure he had easy access to his gun by moving his jacket out of the way and resting his hand on it as he approached the vehicle. When he was twenty feet away the passenger door suddenly flew open and someone got out. Rob started to draw his gun but could see the person had their hands in the air.

"Hey!" a male voice called out.

Rob pushed the gun back into his holster but left his hand on it in case the guy did something stupid. Using his left hand, Rob pulled the Surefire from its nylon holster and used it to light up the area at the guy's feet. He didn't want to irritate the man by shining it directly into his face. Rob could now see the man was white, tall, and skinny, wearing business attire, including a tie.

"Hey, what's up?" Rob asked. *You would think after a full day of sitting here he would have at least taken off the tie.*

"Not much. I've been sitting here for a day already waiting for help to come, but you're the first person I've seen."

"Waiting for help?" Rob asked, puzzled. "Were you able to call for help?"

"No, my phone stopped working when my Tahoe died," the man answered.

Rob waited a second for the man to elaborate on what he meant by waiting for help. When he stayed quiet Rob asked, "If you weren't able to call for help, how is anyone supposed to know that you need help and, more importantly, where to find you?"

"Well... I... Umm..." He stuttered for a moment, confused, before answering, "I just figured the cops or someone would come by at some point to help me out I guess. I started really worrying when the sun went down again and I hadn't seen anyone all day."

Rob finally realized the guy was just expecting help to come to him with no effort on his own part. "Buddy let me tell you something," Rob said, somewhat exasperated. "Help is not going to just magically appear to save you. There is no one coming to help you. If you haven't realized, not only is your car and cell phone not working, but if you walk a couple hundred feet that way," Rob was pointing back towards Moreno Valley," everything you can see is blacked out."

"What do you mean 'blacked out'?" He sounded as if he didn't believe what Rob was saying.

"Blacked. Out. As in, the power is out. No lights, no electricity. Nothing," Rob said sharply.

"Seriously?" The man asked incredulously as he started walking towards the crest of the hill. While the man was gone Rob peaked into the Chevy Tahoe. It was new, top of the line, all the bells and whistles, the best package money could buy. There was a briefcase on the passenger floorboard and a garment bag hanging in the back window. *Nice ride. Too bad he didn't pay for the "hardened against EMP" option,* Rob thought with amusement. He waited several minutes for the man to return and was about to just walk away when Rob finally heard him approaching. "How long has the power been out?" the business man asked, sounding as if he was on the verge of panic.

"Since your car and cell phone stopped working, about twenty-four hours ago," Rob responded. "You didn't think it was odd that you waited here all day, on a street that normally carries hundreds of cars back and forth during the day, but you never saw anyone?"

"Well yeah... but..." The man trailed off.

"But you never decided to do anything about it." It was a statement, not a question, from Rob as he shook his head. *This guy has no hope of surviving.* "Listen, I suggest you get what you can from your car and start walking home."

"Walk home? But I live in San Diego, I'll never be able to walk all that way," he replied with dismay in his voice.

"Well, good luck to you then," Rob said as he started to walk away. He was done dealing with someone who had no desire to help themselves. *How can anyone sit here for almost twenty-four hours and not even walk the short distance to the top of the hill to try to look for help? Unbelievable.*

"No, wait!" The business man shouted, now in a full panic, as he started walking towards Rob while waving his arms. "You have to help me!"

"Stop!" Rob commanded loudly as he pointed the Surefire directly at the man's face.

The business man stopped immediately and covered his eyes. "What the hell? Stop that, it hurts!" he yelled hysterically.

Rob lowered the light to the man's torso. "Listen closely to me," Rob said firmly. "I don't have to do anything, and that includes helping you. What I am going to do is keep walking.

What you do is your own business, but you need to get it in your head that you're on your own now. A tow truck is not coming to tow your Tahoe. A taxi isn't coming to pick you up. The cops aren't coming to save the day. You need to man up and make it happen yourself." With that, Rob turned and started walking north again, leaving the stunned business man standing next to his SUV. *That's the problem with modern society. Everyone depends on someone else for help. No one is self-reliant anymore. Everything is someone else's job. Car has a flat? Call a tow truck. Grass needs mowed? Hire a landscaper. Don't want to clean the house? Hire a housekeeper. Neighbor looked at you weird while their dog pooped on your lawn? Call 9-1-1 and the cops will solve your problems.* There wasn't anything wrong with hiring someone to do something for you if you had the money, but it was breeding a culture in America of relying on everyone else to handle your issues.

Before he was out of ear shot Rob thought he heard the man sobbing. Rob shook his head in disgust. One thing the man said did stick with Rob though. *He's been there almost twenty-four hours and hasn't seen one person go through. I'm not sure if that's a good or a bad thing.* The canyons he was walking through carried hundreds, maybe even thousands, of cars back and forth each day. Most of them were people who worked on one side of the canyons but lived on the other and made the winding commute almost daily. *Then again, maybe it's because the time the EMP hit. No one would have any reason to walk through if they were already at home, unlike me who was at work.*

The road exited on the other side of the hill and the shear walls on both sides fell away and turned into hills which slowly grew further apart the farther he walked. Rob followed the road as it twisted and turned and dropped in elevation. As he rounded the last curve in the road, right before it straightened into a mile long straightaway, a reflection caught his eye from the right side of the road. After a quick check to make sure the business man wasn't following him Rob moved closer to check it out.

When he got to the edge of the road Rob could see a light color sedan on its roof about fifty feet off the roadway. Using his Surefire to light the way, Rob carefully made his way down the embankment, through the flattened brush, and over to the car where he knelt to check inside and found there was one occupant. A white female, probably in her fifties, still in the driver seat being held up by the seat belt. Rob could see right away that she was dead; her skin had a gray pallor to it, eyes were open but unseeing, and her hair was matted with coagulated blood, with a large puddle of it directly underneath her on the roof of the car.

Rob didn't bother checking for any supplies he could use. There was no way he was going to disturb her last place of rest. He got back up and walked back to the road, using the Surefire to study the damage the car left between the roadway and where it came to a rest. Based on the tire marks on the street and the line of damage from the street to where the car came to a rest, Rob figured she was driving downhill when the EMP occurred. Because of the power loss to the car she was unable to maintain control and the car left the roadway, flipped, rolled several times, and came to a rest on its roof. He hoped her death had been quick, with no suffering. *The really sad thing is any family she has will never know what happened to her. All they know is everything stopped working and she never made it home. I can't imagine not making it home and Monica never knowing what happened to me.* It was a sobering thought.

Rob got back onto the road and continued north along the straightaway. He knew there were three or four ranch houses on the right set back off the road towards the end of the mile-long straight section of roadway just before it reached the intersection with San Timoteo Canyon Rd. He stuck to the left shoulder as he walked, keeping an eye out for lights or movement, and an ear out for sounds not produced by nature. As he walked he pulled an apple and a banana from his Eberlestock backpack and ate them on the move.

When Rob reached the T-intersection of Redlands Boulevard and San Timoteo Canyon Road he turned left and headed west. He would have to go west for about a mile before he could turn onto Live Oak Canyon Road, which would take him east towards Yucaipa. He would have gone straight north from the T-intersection and cut through the wilderness, but there were steep hills blocking any access.

After a half mile, a set of railroad tracks curved in from the north and paralleled along the north side of the street. Rob knew this line was one of the main east/west rail lines between southern California and the rest of the country with goods from all over the world being shipped into the Port of Los Angeles and the Port of Long Beach, the two busiest ports in the United States, then put on rail cars to be moved to the rest of the country. Because of that, large trains passed through every thirty minutes. A few years prior Rob was talking to a railroad employee and he told Rob that whenever this line was shut down, due to maintenance or derailment, the rail company lost an estimated one million dollars in revenue for every hour the line was shut down.

As Rob walked he could see a train was stopped on the tracks and blocking the railroad crossing on Live Oak Canyon, where Rob was going to turn. Instead of waiting to get to the intersection to navigate the train, he stepped off the road and walked up the slight embankment to where two of the train cars were attached together. He carefully climbed over the hitch and came out on the other side of the train where he walked west next to the tracks, shoes crunching through the gravel.

When Rob reached Live Oak Canyon he turned right and crossed a small bridge that was built over what was usually a dry creek bed but would fill with water during rain storms. The road then made a few turns before straightening back out and heading straight east for about a mile. This area would be more populated than the area of the canyon he had already walked through, however the houses were all set on large properties and were mainly ranches and small farms that were set back at least a few hundred feet off the roadway. When he reached the last turn he could see several cars sitting sideways in the roadway where the straightaway began. *Roadblock,* Rob thought.

He stopped and studied the area, hoping to figure out if the roadblock was meant to keep people out of the area or meant to create a chokepoint for ambushes. As he looked a female voice suddenly bellowed out from the darkness, "ROAD'S CLOSED!"

Not an ambush then, they would have never said anything before attacking me, they're just trying to keep people out. Maybe I can talk my way through, Rob thought. "Permission to approach?" Rob yelled back.

Rob waited half a minute before he got a response. "Slowly," the female voice said. "And keep your hands where we can see them."

He slowly walked towards the cars, hands held out to his side palms facing forward. *I hope they don't have itchy trigger fingers. Please don't shoot me, please don't shoot me, please don't shoot me.* When Rob reached the cars, he stopped.

"Step to your left between those two cars and come around to the other side. You do anything I don't like, and you will be shot," he heard her say. Her voice was rock steady.

Rob complied and when he reached the other side of the roadblock he paused again to wait for more instructions. He heard movement from his right and a few seconds later a figure, carrying an AR-15 in a low ready position, moved out of the trees on the side of the road and walked slowly towards him. When the figure reached the asphalt of the roadway a flashlight clicked on and was pointed at Rob's mid-section. He appreciated that it wasn't shined in his eyes.

"My partner told you road was closed," a gruff male voice said.

At least two of them then, Rob told himself. "I heard her, but I'm hoping you can make an exception."

"Why would I do that?"

"I'm trying to make it to Yucaipa," Rob responded to the question.

"What's in Yucaipa?" the male voice asked.

"My family." Rob elected to keep his answers as short as the questions.

The line of questioning continued. "Where're you coming from?"

"Work," Rob said.

"Where do you work?"

Rob had a decision to make. Admit he worked in Law Enforcement and risk the people at the roadblock were part of the small section of society who blamed all their problems on the police? Or try to lie his way through and risk the man seeing through his lies. Rob decided to take a chance. "I'm a dispatcher, trying to walk home from Riverside."

There was a pause then, "The center off Alessandro?" The gruffness had been replaced with curiosity.

"That's the one," Rob replied, starting to feel better about his decision to remain honest.

"You have your work ID on you?" he asked Rob.

"In my wallet; Left front pocket."

"Okay, very slowly, take it out."

Rob moved with slow and deliberate movements, not wanting to give anyone the impression he was about to make a move they wouldn't like. He retrieved his wallet, more a money and card clip, out of his pocket, took out his agency ID and handed it to the man.

"Guess you ain't lying," the man said after studying the card. He suddenly turned and yelled out, "He's code-4, guys." The man's usage of a police radio code to let others know Rob wasn't a threat wasn't lost on Rob.

"You Law Enforcement?" Rob asked him.

"Retired two years ago. Colton PD, twenty-nine years. I'm Jim Bowman," The man stuck out his hand, now sounding friendly.

Rob shook it, "Rob Miller." He could now see the man was a six-foot-tall thin black man wearing eye glasses and a load bearing vest with several magazines and medical supplies attached to it. By this time several others were joining them behind the roadblock. "Thanks for not shooting me guys," Rob greeted them. He received a few chuckles in return.

"C'mon over here Rob, take a load off," Jim said to Rob. To the rest of the group he said, "Back to your post's everyone, fun's over."

Rob followed Jim a couple hundred feet down the road where he found several lawn chairs set up in a rough circle. Rob dropped his backpack in one and sat in another, feeling the relief in his feet and knees. "You guys seem to be doing okay here," Rob said.

"Yeah we aren't doing too bad yet. All the neighbors in this area know each other and are pretty self-reliant. Guess it's a result of rural living. It was easy to get everyone organized once I convinced them that this wasn't a short-term blackout. Then we all started preparing. The first thing we did was set up the roadblocks, this one here and one on the east side. We plan to reinforce them but figured the cars would do for now. Luckily a few of the ranches have older equipment so we have a couple tractors that still work, including an old pickup truck that we have been using to help get everyone back and forth from their houses to their shifts at the roadblocks," Jim explained, a touch of pride in his voice.

"Yeah, I guess you guys are on the right track. If nothing else, you're organized," Rob said. He decided to fish for information, "Any of you hear any news from anywhere else?"

"Chuck, one of the neighbors, has an old battery powered radio. I think it only survived because it was down in his basement in an old metal storage trunk. But anyways, the only thing we've heard is one of those emergency alert system messages on repeat from the feds. It just says that they're working on getting the power restored and asking everyone to have patience. It also tells everyone to stay home and help their neighbors if they're able to. Then it repeats. Bunch of bullshit if you ask me," Jim said, now with disgust in his voice. "Sure wish someone in our group had a working ham radio."

"Yeah, probably the only way to get or give any info right now."

"Probably gonna be that way for a long time," Jim agreed.

"Yeah," Rob said, then changed topics. "Hey, I don't know how much you guys have scouted around, but you know the tracks to the west that run along San Timoteo right?"

"Yeah, what about 'em?" Jim asked.

"There's a train stopped on the tracks," Rob could see that bit of information caught Jim's full attention. "I figure when the locomotives lost power, the air brakes lost pressure and they auto stopped the train. I'm no authority on what trains carry, but there might be stuff on there that will help you guys out."

Jim sat thinking for a minute. "Yeah you might be right. First light I'll organize a group to go check it out. Thanks for letting me know. I'm sure we would have come across it at some point, but it would be nice to get to it before anyone else does." Jim changed the conversation. "Hey, you know James Blackman?"

"Tall white guy, goes by JB?"

"Yeah that's him," Jim replied with a smile. "How's he doing? We went to the academy together."

"He's good. He's commander over the southwest division now. I heard he's planning on retiring next year. Or was, I guess, before all this happened."

"He promoted that high?" Jim asked with a short laugh. "Guess I shouldn't be surprised, he's a good guy. Really smart too. If I remember right, he took the award for top academic in our academy class."

"Yeah, he is," Rob agreed. They ended up talking for another thirty minutes, with Jim asking about many of the officers that worked for Rob's agency. Law enforcement was a tight knit community and it was common for officers and employees of one agency to become close friends with the officers and employees of other agencies. Rob finally decided he had delayed enough. "Hey, listen, thanks for letting me walk through. I really appreciate it. It would have sucked to have to try to walk down to Redlands or up to Beaumont before circling back to Yucaipa."

"No problem Rob," Jim said. "Just follow the road. If you start to wander one of the neighbors might shoot you, all of us are armed and protecting our own houses in addition to the roadblocks. Our eastern roadblock is set up at the end of those S-turns, west of the bridge that cuts across that dry creek bed. It's manned twenty-four hours just like this one. Right now, the guy in charge over there is Will Hall. He's a retired Marine chopper pilot, good people. As you approach the roadblock make sure you're making some noise, so they don't think you're trying to sneak up on 'em. Let them know I let you through over here and you shouldn't have any problems on that side."

Rob stood up and shouldered his backpack, then stuck out his hand, "Thanks again Jim. Good luck to you, I hope you and your people here make it through all this without too much trouble."

"No problem Rob," Jim shook Rob's hand. "Good luck to you too. I hope you get home and find your family safe and sound."

With that, Rob got back onto the road and started walking east again. As he walked he could feel the temperature was dropping and it was much colder than it was the night before. He zipped up his jacket and pulled his beanie down a little tighter around his ears. *This isn't a bad place to try to survive. It's a long narrow valley that's pretty easy to protect on both ends. On both sides steep hills provide protection from anyone coming from the north or south. They have a lot of good land to farm. I'm sure most of the houses have at least a vegetable garden already. And most of them have horses and cattle, and if I remember right one of the places has a good size heard of cows and sheep. These people are going to be okay if they can protect it all.*

Rob made it through to the S-turns without incident. Once he reached the sharp turns that wound around a few hills he started whistling and clapping every few seconds, taking Jim's advice to make some noise. As he came around the last turn he was confronted with the roadblock. He clapped a few times before putting his hands in the air and yelling out, "Just passing through, Jim Bowman let me walk through. Please don't shoot!"

"Hold it right there! And keep your hands visible," a gravelly male voice yelled out. Rob stopped and waited, hands held out to his side. A minute later a white male in his 60's with a military style haircut and carrying an AR-15 walked up to Rob. "You say Bowman let you through?"

"Yeah, you must be Will Hall," Rob replied.

"That's me. If Jim let you through on the west side I guess you're okay. You must be law enforcement." Rob gave a quick nod, so Will continued, "He always had a hard on for you blue line fellas." It almost sounded like an insult, but Ron noticed the smile on Will's face and knew he was joking.

"Better than a hard on for the big green weenie," Rob joked back, alluding to the Marine Corps.

"Touché," Will said with a laugh. He turned and raised his voice, "One coming through, he's headed east." He turned back to Rob, "You're good to go. Carry on."

"Thanks," Rob said with a respectful nod before walking up to, then through, the makeshift roadblock. Will was the only one Rob could see, but he knew there were probably several other keeping a sharp watch.

He left the roadblock behind, continued following the road, and a few minutes later came to the bridge that Jim had mentioned. It crossed a narrow deep ravine created by a creek that flowed through whenever it was raining in the area. It was part of the same creek bed Rob had crossed just before reaching the first roadblock and Jim Bowman.

He decided to take a break and get some food in his stomach. Rob walked off the north side of the roadway and along the ravine for a couple hundred feet before he came to an area where the wall of the ravine was shallow enough that he could easily hike down to the creek bed. Since being hired as a dispatcher Rob drove through this area several times a week and he knew there were a lot of trees and bushes in the ravine that he could use for cover. He hiked down then turned and followed the creek bed in a northeasterly direction until he came across a grove of trees. He found a suitable tree and took his pack off then sat on the soft sandy ground and leaned back.

Rob checked his watch. 4:12 am. He decided to just relax for ten minutes before eating. It felt good to rest after the long walk. While he was resting Rob heard rustling in the brush to his right. He slowly and quietly sat up, slid the Marlin .22 off the side of the backpack, and slowly pulled back then pushed forward on the bolt to quietly chamber a round. He waited a few minutes then heard the rustling again. Rob quietly took the Surefire out of its holder, activated the light, and pointed it in the direction of the noise. A rabbit. It scampered back into the brush. Rob left the flashlight on and put it on top of his bag with it angled towards where the rabbit disappeared, then shouldered the rifle and waited patiently.

Three minutes later the rabbit came back out of the brush on the right edge of the Surefire's light beam. Rob aimed using the iron sites, took a breath, slowly let it out, and gently pressed the trigger. The .22 round fired with a loud snapping sound but almost no recoil. Not as loud as his Springfield XD when fired, but anyone in the immediate area would know a gun was just fired. The round hit the rabbit in the neck, knocking it over and killing it instantly. Rob chambered another round, set the rifle on safe, laid it across his backpack, then went over and picked up the rabbit.

Rob had a couple hours before the sun came up and wanted to clear the area due to the sound of the gunshot. His hunger would have to wait a while longer. Using the Gerber folding knife he quickly skinned and gutted the rabbit, then used a piece of paracord and hung it from the bottom of his backpack. He used some sand from the ground to dry the rabbit blood from his hands, slung the backpack on, picked up the Marlin rifle, and headed out. He wanted to keep the rifle handy in case he came across anymore rabbits.

Instead of climbing back out of the ravine and using the road, he decided to stick to the creek bed as it would lead him in the direction he needed to go, northeast. He knew it would lead him to the edge of the city limits of Yucaipa and Rob was confident he could find a place to climb out when the time came. His progress was slowed some by piles of debris and the soft sand of the creek bed, but Rob pressed on, walking around, over, and sometimes through the obstacles created by brush and debris. He passed more groups of trees and kept his eyes open for more rabbits.

At one point as he walked Rob heard a string of gunshots, probably eight or nine in a row. Being in the ravine, he couldn't determine which direction they came from, but they sounded far away. *Hell, that could have been fireworks for all I know, but who would be setting off fireworks at a time like this? I hope Jim Bowman's people are okay.*

Rob came to a large fork in the ravine. The left side went almost directly north. The right continued northeast. He figured the one on the left was the same one that ran underneath the I-10 freeway further north and continued through the middle of Yucaipa, and the one on the right most likely intersected with Live Oak Canyon Rd before continuing east, paralleling the I-10 on the south side of the freeway. Rob decided to go right. He lived near the east edge of Yucaipa and wanted to avoid residential areas as much as possible and the right fork would stay closer to the route he was thinking about taking.

Rob walked for another thirty minutes before deciding to stop and make camp. It wasn't quite 6:00 am and he had about one more hour of darkness. He wanted to have his camp setup and the rabbit cooked before it got too light, so he found another small grove of trees and put his backpack down.

First things first, he though as he pulled the Kershaw Camp 10 machete out of the sheath strapped to the backpack and started clearing some of the brush to make a small clearing he could use to sleep. Once he had a suitable area cleared he pulled a five by five dark green tarp from his backpack and used some paracord to tie it above to give himself some shade.

Rob also rigged up an early warning system. He wasn't so much concerned with human predators down in the ravine, but he knew coyotes were often spotted by the residents in the area and they might be curious by the smell of cooked rabbit. He used paracord and started at the wall of the ravine about twenty feet from where he would sleep then strung the paracord about a foot and a half from the ground, making a half circle around his camp and ending at the ravine wall on the other side of his camp. Before he went to sleep he would tie the metal canteen holder to the paracord and put a handful of small rocks in it. The idea was if someone or something approached his camp they would trip the paracord which would cause the canteen holder to knock over, making noise with the rocks inside, and giving him a few seconds to wake up and get ready to confront the potential threat.

Once he was done with the early warning system he took the empty energy drink can from his Eberlestock backpack and started making a crude rocket stove. He cut the top off the sixteen-ounce can and created several holes in the side near the bottom for airflow. For fuel, he gathered some dead grass, twigs, and small branches and took them over to his camp. He stabilized the can in the soft sand then put some of the dead grass into the bottom of the can, and using a water proof match from his backpack he lit it on fire and the dry grass started burning immediately. Rob fed a handful of twigs and some more grass into it, then started adding pieces of small branches from the small pile of supplies he gathered.

Once Rob was certain the fire was not going to go out he untied the rabbit from his backpack and used the Gerber folding knife to cut pieces of the meat off. He pulled both of the tomatoes he still had left from the farmer's market and cut them into large cubes. He put the rabbit meat and tomato into the tin canteen holder and added some of his precious water, then, using the rocket stove, he boiled the rabbit and tomato stew for about twenty minutes. After letting the stew cool, he bit into one of the pieces of meat to confirm it was cooked through and found it was firm with no juices running out. Perfect. Rob enjoyed his first hot meal in what felt like a lifetime. He took out the plastic water bottle, still full after being filled by Rachel before leaving her house, and drank half of it, then used it to refill the water pouch. Once he was done the water bottle had about a liter and a half. After he finished the bottle he would be down to his water pouch and what was left in his canteen. *Hopefully it's enough to see me home.*

Rob put out the fire in the rocket stove by pouring sand in the top and smothering it. He wanted to make a fire for warmth but knew the sun was about to come up and he wouldn't need it anyways in about an hour. Plus, he didn't want to draw any attention to himself. Not wanting to give any coyotes any more reason to check his camp out, he picked up the remains from dinner and walked them a couple hundred yards back down the ravine and buried them in a shallow hole. Being buried so shallow wouldn't stop coyotes from finding the guts, but it might cause them to make some noise while they dug, hopefully alerting Rob to their presence. When he arrived back at camp he put some small rocks into the metal canteen holder and tied it off to the paracord early warning system.

Before laying down he tried to clean himself up as best he could. He used the bandana Rachel used in the plane crash smoke, poured a little bit of water on it, and used it to wipe himself down. He also used a small disposable toothpick with floss attached at the end to clean his teeth. *Not exactly a hot bath and cleaning at the dentist, but it will do for now.* The last thing he did was take off his shoes and socks to let them dry out and checked his feet for sores and blisters. His feet were holding up well. He rubbed them for a minute then laid down in his small clearing, using his backpack as a pillow. The sky was starting to lighten. 7:07 am. He listened to the sounds of nature, mainly birds chirping, that were no longer suppressed by the sounds of man and all things mechanical, and slowly faded from consciousness.

Rob slept fitfully, coming fully awake every thirty minutes to an hour and checking his surroundings before dozing off again. He did this till 1:00 pm and decided he wasn't going to get anymore sleep so he pulled the picture of his wife and son out of his pocket and stared at it for a few minutes, quietly praying for their safety.

Rob put the picture away and suddenly felt lonely. Down in the ravine, no sounds other than the chirping of some birds, Rob felt like the last man on earth. Even though logically he knew he was far from the last, he couldn't help but feel like he was it. He desperately missed his family, and now had a better appreciation for having a partner to walk with. Not just for safety, but for companionship. Having walked with Rachel the night before he now knew firsthand the value of having someone he could talk to and confide in, someone to break up the monotony of the journey, someone to watch his back, someone to just talk to. Rob took a deep breath, pulled himself out of his funk, and started to get ready to move.

He checked his feet one more time then pulled his last pair of clean socks from his backpack, put them on, and laced up his shoes. He pulled the Kershaw Siege and roll of toilet paper out of the backpack, walked to the other side of the creek bed, found a bush, dug a hole, and did his business. As he was going, he realized the sky was cloudy. Not just a few white clouds high in the sky, but thick dark cloud cover. The kind that indicated it was going to rain, and rain hard. *When did the clouds move in? The sky was clear when I first laid down this morning. If it was cloudy it would have been obvious with the aurora.* He racked his brain but couldn't remember what the recent forecasts said about rain.

When he finished he covered up the hole then went back to his camp and realized the bottom of a ravine probably wasn't the best place to be if it did start raining. That little epiphany got him moving and he quickly took down the early warning system and tarp, got everything stowed away, put the Marlin .22 into its makeshift holder, put the backpack on, and started walking quickly up the ravine. He scanned the walls on both sides while he walked, looking for a way to climb up and out, but so far, the walls were straight up and down. As he walked he continued to dodge piles of debris and lots of brush. Now, the piles of debris weren't just an obstacle, they were a reminder of the amount of water that moved through here at times. At one point he came to an area where the ravine narrowed and was blocked by thick brush. Rob almost turned back but knew he had a long distance to cover before reaching an area he could climb out, so he pulled the machete from its sheath and started hacking. He cleared about ten feet before the brush suddenly ended and he was able to continue walking.

Ten minutes later Rob came to the spot where the ravine met back up with Live Oak Canyon Rd. Instead of a bridge to allow cars to cross over the creek, whoever built the road made what was effectively a concrete dam with two large metal pipes coming through. The cars utilizing the road would drive over the dam and any water could pass under the roadway via the two pipes. Rob could see water coming through the pipes. It wasn't much more than would come out of a large garden hose, but Rob knew that could change to a torrent in an instant. *Must be raining in the hills.* Looking around he found a dirt trail that started at the bottom and angled up the wall before letting out near the roadway. It was steep but had plenty of rocks he could use to climb.

He started to walk over when he paused. He could use the water coming from the drain pipes to refill the plastic water bottles. It wouldn't be clean water, but he had a personal use water filter he could use. He turned back to the pipes as he pulled both bottles from the backpack. After drinking the last of the clean water from the water bottle, he went over to the pipes and filled each one. It only took a few minutes but by the time he was done the water was flowing much faster. It wouldn't be long before the dry creek bed became a torrent of water. He put the smaller water bottle into the backpack and carried the gallon container as he made his way to the trail leading out of the ravine where he climbed to the top, using the rocks to help his ascent.

Once he was close to the top Rob stopped and looked around, checking the surroundings and getting his bearings. He was much closer to the I-10 freeway than he thought he would be. Half a mile or less. Rob needed to decide which route he would take through Yucaipa and eventually home. There were numerous different ways he could go that would ultimately end with him being home, but which one was the safest? *I can take Live Oak all the way up or take Live Oak then use Avenue E to head east. Taking Live Oak all the way, or even cutting onto Avenue E probably isn't the best, both of those go through a lot of neighborhoods. If I take the freeway I can follow it east, then hop over where it starts to turn south towards Calimesa and Beaumont. I can come out onto Avenue G and make my way east using the canyon it cuts through. The good thing about that canyon is there are plenty of trees most of the way up which I can use for cover, and if I take that all the way up, I'll only be a couple miles from home.* No matter which route he took he would end up walking through some neighborhoods, but Avenue G and the canyon it ran through would be the best way to avoid most of them.

Rob looked at his watch. 1:58 pm. He'd rather not walk in daylight, but with the coming rain and possible freezing nighttime temperatures that would come with it, he wanted to get as far as possible. Before heading out again Rob took a black hooded rain poncho from his backpack, rolled it into a ball, and put it in his jacket pocket. He wanted to be ready if the skies released their moisture, which at this point looked inevitable.

He took one last look around then got up and started walking. He crossed the street and walked towards the freeway. Situated just south of the freeway on the east side of Live Oak Canyon was a large farm. During Fall the owner turned it into a pumpkin patch, then into a Christmas tree farm after Thanksgiving. When Rob came to the parking lot he hopped the short swinging cross bar that blocked vehicles from accessing it during the off season. He crossed the large parking lot and walked through the small kiosk buildings that normally served as a ticket booth and concession stand then moved into the large open area where the carnival rides were normally set up and cut through, heading east.

Rob moved onto a dirt road that skirted the perimeter of the farm and ran along the same ravine he had climbed out of on the other side of the roadway. As he walked he came to a large green barn set on the north side of the dirt road, Rob decided to check it out. He walked up to the large doors on the front of the building and tried to push them open. They started to move but then met resistance. Locked. He walked around the building and found a pedestrian door on the right side. He tried the door knob, but it was also locked.

Rob took a good look and decided to force it. *The door frame looks old. Only the knob, no dead bolt. Should be easy enough, and there might be something inside I can use. Like a race car,* he chuckled at his own joke as he stepped back and took one more look around. He dropped his backpack and gallon of water next to the door then kicked the door using his right leg, driving forward with his left. He made contact just to the side of the door knob and the door shot open, the frame splintering and giving way on the first try.

Instead of entering right away Rob stepped to the side, drew his gun, and waited. He wanted to give anyone who might be inside time to make a move and give themselves away. After a couple minutes with no movement or sound from inside Rob stepped away from the doorway and quickly transitioned to the other side, watching the interior as he moved. The inside was dark, but Rob could see nothing that concerned him, so he stepped through and started clearing the interior, using the weapon light only when necessary. He moved clockwise through the large room and checked under and behind everything. Once he confirmed everything was clear he holstered the gun, pulled his flashlight out, turned on, and got his first good look of the inside of the barn.

The walls were lined with tools and miscellaneous things Rob assumed were useful in running and maintaining a farm and pumpkin patch, but what caught his eye though was in the center of the barn. An aging, but well maintained, green tractor and several pieces of farming attachments. *I wonder if it still runs. If it does, a tractor will be invaluable to have once things settle down. If it works I can pull one of the sparkplugs so someone else can't take it, then come back for it later when I need it.*

Rob climbed up into the cab of the tractor and looked around for a key. He had never driven a tractor in the past but figured he could cross that bridge when he needed to. He looked through the cab, in the visor, under the seat, every nook and cranny he could find, but couldn't find a key. He got back down and started searching, first through the shelves lining the walls, then through the drawers and toolboxes lining the large work benches. He looked for fifteen minutes and couldn't find anything. *The owner probably takes them home with him, wherever that is. I'm never going to find them. I should have learned to hotwire.*

Rob decided to not waste any more time in the barn and started to leave, but as he approached the door to retrieve his backpack something to the right side of the door on the wall caught his eye. A keyholder was mounted to the wall, with around twenty-five keys on various keyrings hanging from the hooks. *Really? I'm so dumb,* Rob thought as he shook his head. *That's the first place I should have looked.* He didn't know what a tractor key would look like, *would it look like a standard car key? House key? Master lock key?*

He grabbed all of them and walked back to the tractor, climbed back in, sat down, and started looking at the keys. He immediately discarded about half of them, seeing they were too small to fit the key hole on the dash. With a dozen keys left he started trying them one by one, finding the correct one on his fifth try. He dropped the rest of the keys on the floorboard, put the correct key into the ignition, and turned it one position to the right. The lights on the dash immediately lit up. *Well, that might not even be promising, since the cars back at dispatch still had working lights.*

He said a small prayer, took a deep breath, and turned the key all the way to the right. Rob almost jumped when the engine turned over. It cranked several times before Rob let go. *Okay, now it's promising. The engine is at least turning over.* Rob used his right foot to push down what looked like a gas pedal, held it halfway down for about a second, then released it. *Here goes nothing,* he thought as he turned the key again. This time the engine cranked twice before it roared to life. Rob gave a shout of joy, let the engine run for about twenty seconds, then shut the tractor off and removed the key. *I can't believe that actually worked. Now I just need to hide the key and pull a spark plug or something so that I can come back later and get it.*

Rob climbed back down from the tractor, reached back into the cab, and picked up all the discarded keys. He checked to make sure none of the extra keys looked like they matched the one that worked, then put them all back onto the key hooks next to the door. *Maybe if someone tries to take it and uses these keys they will just give up when none of them fit.*

Rob went back to the tractor and released the clasps holding the engine cover down. He raised the cover and took a good look at the engine. *Wait, its diesel. It doesn't take spark plugs. Okay, what else can I take off that's quick and easy and will be easy to put back on? Maybe if I just unhook the wire leading to the ignition?* He located a green wire that was attached to the engine and led through the fire wall between the engine compartment and the cab in the general area of where the ignition was located and pulled it from the plug it was seated in on the engine side.

He got back into the tractor to make sure it wouldn't start. After several tries and no response from the engine he was satisfied. He went back to the engine compartment and tucked the wire down into the engine block. Next, he got a small screw driver from the toolbox and disconnected both batteries so that they wouldn't drain themselves over the next few months. Rob knew it would probably be awhile before he came back. He closed the engine cover, found some duct tape on the work bench, and used it to tape the key to the inside of the driver side drive tire. *I really doubt someone is going to find it there. That's as good as it gets. If someone knows what they are looking for with that green wire, they probably know enough to hotwire it anyways.*

Before leaving Rob decided to take a few minutes to try to secure the door he kicked in. He noticed two large metal holders mounted to the door frame on each side of the door. *I think those holders are meant to hold a two by four across the door to secure it.* Rob couldn't find a two by four so he found several smaller pieces of wood and jammed them down into the holders, effectively blocking the door shut without locking it using the door knob. *Okay that works, now to get out of here.*

Rob could see a window about ten feet up the wall on the opposite side from where the door was located. He found a ladder that would reach and climbed up. It took some effort, the window had been in the closed position for a long time, but Rob was able to get it open. The window opened to the inside, so Rob crawled through, hung on to the window sill, reached back in and closed the window as much as he could, then dropped down to the ground. This time he was careful not to let his knees buckle so he didn't have a repeat of the warehouse wall in Moreno Valley.

Rob walked back around to the pedestrian door and gave it a good push. *That's definitely secure. When I come back I think I'm going to have some trouble getting in myself unless someone breaks in before I come back.* Rob picked up his backpack and gallon of water that were still sitting on the ground next to the door and, feeling accomplished, he walked back onto the dirt road and headed east again.

As he walked he looked down into the ravine and could see the amount of water moving through was building. The creek bed was no longer dry, having at least a foot of fast moving water in it. As Rob approached the far east end of the farm property it was as if the flood gates opened. One moment the ground was dry and the next moment he was being pounded by sheets of rain. He quickly put on his rain poncho, pulling it down over his backpack. He purposely bought a large one, knowing he would need it to cover his backpack if he wanted to keep everything as dry as possible, and was glad to see that it covered the rifle as well.

As the rain continued to pound him his elation at finding the tractor was slowly replaced by irritation at the weather. Normally weather never affected his mood as he figured he had no control over it, so it was something to just deal with, weather hot or cold wet or dry, but due to his current situation his mood turned sour.

Rob continued to walk, now through mud and water, and was grateful he had the Merrell hiking shoes on as they gave him good traction in the muck. He reached the area where the road curved slightly north towards the freeway then looped back west along the north perimeter of the farm property, just south of the freeway, and found a large gap in the fence line that looked like it was created when heavy rainfall washed out a large portion of the ground and took the fence with it.

He walked through and hopped the guardrail, then moved onto the I-10 freeway. He crossed the three eastbound lanes of the freeway, hopped the two guardrails and pushed through the bushes that served as the center divider on this portion of the freeway, then entered the westbound lanes. He turned and started walking eastbound, entering Yucaipa while enduring some of the heaviest rain he could remember hitting this area.

CHAPTER 8

As Rob walked through the torrential rainfall he debated, *Should I keep going, or find someplace to hunker down until the worst of this passes? I really want to get home but walking through this cold rain is starting to suck.* As he wrestled with this question he noticed a car stopped on the shoulder of the freeway about one hundred feet ahead of him. He stopped and tried to determine if anyone was inside the car but was unable to due to the reduced visibility caused by the torrential rainfall. Through the rain he could see it was an SUV and possibly had a roof rack but he wasn't able to make out any other details. Knowing the rain would give any occupants the same issues with visibility as it was giving himself, he decided to slowly approach.

Rob was within twenty-five feet of the car when he realized, *That's not a roof rack, that's a lightbar.* Another ten feet and he could see the SUV was a black and white police unit belonging to the California Highway Patrol. Rob walked up to the SUV and looked through the windows. Empty. He could see the double gun lock situated between the two front seats that normally held a shotgun and a patrol rifle were empty.

I should check inside, never know what I might find that could help me out. Rob took a step back from then made a circuit around the unit as he looked around. The rain was still coming down hard and limiting visibility, but he still checked as much as he could, trying to see if the police officer who was driving the unit was still in the area. When he didn't see anyone out and about he tried the doors, but they were all locked.

Hopefully the cop it belongs to is long gone and isn't going to walk up as I'm doing this, Rob thought to himself as he pulled up the rain poncho, took his backpack off, and removed the Kershaw Siege. One swing of the hatchet and he was in, accessing through the driver side door. Rob reached in, unlocked the doors using the button next to window controls, pulled the door open, and leaned inside. He quickly looked through the compartments he could reach and found nothing useful.

Rob moved around to the passenger side and opened the door, repeating the process of checking. Still nothing. He knew there would probably be nothing in the back seat as that is where prisoners are transported but he checked just to make sure, then made his way to the back cargo area where he found a large black metal box with several locking drawers. They were all unlocked, and Rob found them empty except for a few stacks of paperwork and some traffic collision reconstruction equipment. *Oh well, it was worth checking.*

Using the cover created by the raised rear door of the SUV, Rob quickly stowed the Kershaw Siege in his backpack, made sure his rain poncho was on correctly, and was about to walk away when he realized the unit could still help him. *This rain hasn't lightened up at all, it might even be coming down harder than before. This unit is perfect shelter.* Rob went back to the passenger side, quickly pulled off his rain poncho and backpack, tossed them and the gallon of water he still carried into the center console area onto the now useless radio equipment, then got in and closed the door. Rob sighed. It was a relief to be out of the pounding rain. *I wonder what that ravine looks like now. I dodged a bullet with that one. This is nice though.* Rob just sat and relaxed for several minutes, trying to decompress.

Rob checked his watch. 2:38 pm. *Hopefully this rain doesn't last long, I want to get going.* To help pass the time Rob first drank some water and ate two apples and a banana. He now had one apple and some of the grapes left over from what he was able to scavenge from the farmer's market in Moreno Valley along with two and a half bags of mixed nuts, three 5-hour energy shots, and one BANG energy drink left over from the Chevron gas station he and Rachel had broken into.

Once he ate he decided to do an inventory of his backpack to make sure his supplies were dry. He checked through each compartment and pouch, doing a quick visual inspection of all his supplies, and found the Eberlestock was holding up as advertised. *This pack was well worth the money,* Rob thought when he found everything was dry. *Of course, the rain poncho did most of the work, but still.*

After checking his backpack and making sure everything was situated in case he had to make a hasty exit, Rob pulled out the picture of his wife and son. He stared at the picture and started to wonder if he would ever see them again. Rob's mind started wandering and entered a dark place with different scenarios running through his mind. The house catching fire; looters breaking in; a plane crashing directly into the house. *Stop thinking like that!* Rob told himself. *They are going to be fine. Monica is more than capable of handling any issue that might come up. I'm going to be home before I know it and find all my worrying was for nothing.*

Rob forced himself to think of better things. He reminisced about the trip they took shortly after Jackson was born. Rob's family who were in Arizona lived in a town known as Sierra Vista and when Jackson was only one month old they made the seven-hour drive to surprise Rob's family who thought it would be several more months before they met the newest addition to the family. Predictably Rob's family was ecstatic and smothered Jackson with love. They spent four days before returning back to California. It was one of the best trips of Rob's life.

Rob leaned his head back and closed his eyes, enjoying the

sound of rain hitting the roof of the police car. He was feeling sleepy after the broken sleep he endured that morning in the ravine and without knowing it Rob fell into a deep sleep where he had the same recurring nightmare he couldn't wake up from. In it he was walking into his neighborhood looking forward to reuniting with his family and as he was turning onto his street a plane suddenly plummeted out of the sky and landed directly on his house. In the implausible way dreams sometimes happened, he could hear his wife and son screaming for help even though the entire house was gone. And no matter how hard he ran, it was as if he was running in place, unable to get any closer to the house.

He finally awoke with a violent jerk and sat forward, breathing hard and trying to get his bearings. It took him a few seconds to come back to reality, but once he was fully alert Rob decided to get moving right away. The rain had abated and was just barely misting at this point, but even if the rain was still coming down like it was earlier, Rob would have set out. After that nightmare he wanted to get home as soon as possible. He rolled the rain poncho into a ball and put it into his jacket pocket then got out of the police car, pulling his backpack and gallon of water out behind him. Before he put the backpack on he pulled one of the 5-hour energy shots out and quickly downed it, then he started walking east, sticking to the westbound lanes of the I-10 freeway. He looked at his watch. 4:28 pm. *I slept almost two hours. I needed it but that was way more time than I wanted to waste.*

A quarter mile further east there was a state-run rest area situated on the south side of the freeway, connecting to the eastbound lanes. Rob knew it was a regular stop for long haul truck drivers and people traveling in cars and during the overnight hours it was regularly at capacity or even fuller. With the EMP occurring sometime around midnight Rob expected to see numerous cars and big rigs parked there, but even then he was surprised by the amount of people he could see. There were large groups of men, women, and children in the parking lots around the cars and in the grassy areas around the buildings that housed the bathrooms and vending machines. Rob estimated there were at least one hundred, and possibly closer to one hundred and fifty people, at the rest stop. Most of the kids were playing games like tag and catch, using a few footballs and baseballs, while most of the adults were in several groups of varying sizes talking amongst themselves.

As he walked, someone in the rest stop caught sight of him and alerted everyone else of Rob's presence. Rob quickly double checked his surroundings, trying to plan out what he would do in any given situation. Dozens of scenarios ran through his head and for each one Rob chose a course of action. He knew that if he had the scenario in mind, when it occurred he would react faster. To his left was the shoulder of the westbound lanes with a four-foot high concrete barrier wall, a few feet of dirt, a six-foot high chain link fence, then the road, Calimesa Boulevard, that ran next to the freeway. On the other side of the street was a home remodel business, then hills. Rob determined all of this in a few seconds. *I should have jumped over to Calimesa when I left that CHP unit. Being on the freeway doesn't give me much room to maneuver if I need to and virtually no cover.*

When he looked back at the rest stop he could see a group of around fifteen men were gathered and pointing at him while talking animatedly. *Must be the self-appointed leaders of the group, let's hope they're smart enough to mind their own business.* Rob could see that several of them carried something in their hands, but he couldn't make out what the objects were. As Rob watched them, and they him, it appeared they came to a decision, as one of the males was now talking with the rest nodding their heads.

Rob grew increasingly certain that they were going to try to do something but what that was, Rob couldn't say. It could be anything from saying hi and trying to get information, to trying to kill Rob and taking what he carried. If Rob was a betting man, he would put money on the latter so he drew his gun and kept putting one foot in front of the other, mentally pleading with the group to stay put and let him continue. Rob's brother Matt had a saying he was fond of, particularly when suspects tried to run or fight with him, and it came to Rob's mind: *Don't start none, won't be none.*

Rob once again checked his side of the freeway then turned and looked at the large group once more. When he did, he could see one in the group, a large white man with a thick beard and wearing a dirty white shirt was lifting a long gun, *looks like a shotgun,* and pointing it in Rob's direction. Rob immediately threw himself to the ground as the shotgun boomed. He heard several small projectiles hit the concrete barrier wall behind him. He turned and looked at the ground next to the part of wall where the projectiles hit and could see several small BB's rolling around on the ground. Several things went through Rob's head. *Birdshot. That idiot is at least fifty yards away and expected to hit me with birdshot.* Rob knew that even if he had been hit the BB's most likely would not have penetrated his jacket, and any BB's that hit his skin would have probably done nothing more than give him some welts without breaking skin.

Rob pushed himself into a crouch and moved several yards to the east, putting a little distance between himself and where the group would have lost visual of him. When he was in the new position Rob popped back up to a standing position, gun already pointed towards the rest area. It took him less than a second to acquire the group of fifteen men in his sights and he could see they were running towards the center divider in the eastbound lanes. Rob fired five times into the group. *I hope I don't hit any of those kids over there,* he thought to himself. Fourteen men dropped to the ground, the fifteenth turned and ran for the buildings in the rest area, and everyone else at the rest stop started running for cover, with children crying and parents screaming for their kids to get down.

As soon as Rob fired the fifth shot, he turned around, took his backpack off, and tossed it over the wall, all in one motion. He quickly followed, placing his left hand on top of the concrete and vaulting over while holding the gun in his right. He left the plastic gallon water container behind knowing it would just slow him down. *Not worth it. I gotta be alive to be thirsty.* As soon as he was over he crouched and put his backpack on, then flinched as gunfire started hitting the wall where he jumped over. It sounded like three or four different calibers.

He started moving east, between the wall and the six-foot fence behind him. He wanted to get over the fence but knew with the fence being higher than the concrete wall the group of men would easily see him and would possibly be close enough to take an effective shot at Rob. He moved about fifteen yards then popped back up, gun aimed in the general direction of where he thought the group would be and could see several heads looking over the bushes in the center of the freeway, each one wielding a gun. Rob fired three more rounds towards them and was rewarded with a scream that caused them all to drop back down. *Nine rounds left.*

Rob turned and ran, not bothering to crouch. He was hoping now that one of their group was hit they would stay down a little longer, or hopefully give up altogether, and he wanted to take advantage of the situation by putting as much distance between them as possible. Rob ran fifty yards before he risked checking behind him. No one. *They must still be on the ground, now's my chance.* Rob threw his backpack over the six-foot fence, holstered his gun, and scrambled over the fence as fast as he could, the whole time expecting to hear more gunfire from the group.

Once he was over Rob stayed low, picked up his backpack, and kept moving east as fast as he could. He was still crouched low trying to stay invisible behind the concrete divider wall when he heard gunfire that sounded as if it was aimed at the area where he jumped over the fence. *At least three different guns,* he thought. *Good thing they didn't open up like that when I was going over the fence. They aren't really that bright.* He followed Calimesa and moved past the T-intersection with Wildwood Canyon.

As Rob ran he pulled a full magazine from the holder on his left, released the partially spent magazine, slammed the full one home, then picked up and placed the partially depleted one into the magazine holder. About one hundred yards past the intersection, the concrete wall ended and turned into a low guard rail. Rob would now have no cover if he kept running. Thinking fast he crouched down next to the end of the wall, pulled the Marlin .22 rifle off his backpack, and used the wall to stabilize the gun he looked down the freeway and waited.

A few minutes later he could see a head pop up and look over the bushes, searching for Rob. Another minute or so and two men pushed through the bushes and onto the westbound lanes. One appeared to be the one with the shotgun that fired the initial round at Rob, the other was also holding what was possibly a rifle or shotgun however Rob was too far away to tell for sure. Rob sighted in on the one with the shotgun and slowly pulled the trigger. The gun fired and both men dropped to the ground. Rob chambered another round and fired again, aiming once more for the one with the shotgun. He waited a few more seconds and when one of the men started looking around Rob fired again. He figured it would give him some extra time to clear the area, time he desperately needed especially as the cover provided by the concrete was now gone, replaced by the guard rail.

Rob turned and ran again, not bothering to take the time to secure the rifle back onto his backpack. He wasn't sure if he had hit either one of the men on the freeway but knew he needed to take advantage of the short amount of time he had while the men were laying on the freeway trying to hide from Rob's rifle fire. The freeway now veered slightly south and moved away from Calimesa, the road that Rob was on. On the left was a senior mobile home park and Rob figured with a bunch of retired people living there he would be safe to run through as long as he kept moving.

He cut left into the main entrance, made a right on the first interior street, and ran for all he was worth, now huffing and puffing, heart feeling like it was going to explode, but pushing through the pain and using the park as cover. As Rob ran he could see curtains moving in windows and a few small dogs barked at him but, other than that, he made it to the last mobile home in the row with no issues. Here, the road curved left and the houses on the left continued, but on the right the houses ended, and the mobile home park property was separated from a large canal buy a low chain link fence. Just to the south of the row of mobile homes was Calimesa, which had a bridge where it crossed over the canal.

Rob hopped the chain link fence, slowly moved south until he reached the street, and could see the line of sight between him and the rest area was mostly obstructed by the terrain. He crossed the street at a crouch and decided to find a spot to hunker down and watch the group to make sure they didn't send a search party after him.

Rob crossed the bridge at a run and came to a car repair business that was situated between the freeway and the street. He took a quick look around and when he didn't spot any people or animals on the grounds, threw his backpack over the gate, slipped the rifle through the gap between the gate and the fence, and quickly followed. After picking up the backpack and rifle he moved to the backside of the property closest to the freeway and found a small storage lot with about twenty cars in it that were waiting for repair. *Never gonna happen now,* Rob thought.

He went to the west side of the lot and chose a pickup truck to use as a lookout. He climbed into the bed of the truck and started watching the freeway and street as his breathing and heartrate finally started to slow. *If I keep having to run like this, I'm going to be ready to give Rachel a run for her money in a foot race.* As he watched for movement he pulled the ammo boxes from his backpack and replaced what had been expended. First the eight 9mm rounds from his XD magazine, then four rounds in the .22 magazine, one of those being the one he used on the rabbit the night before.

As Rob watched he could see several people carry a body from the center divider of the freeway back to the rest stop. *I got at least one.* As he watched they walked back to the westbound lanes and picked up another person and carried them to the rest stop as well. *Guess I got two.* This time he could see it was the guy with the beard and dirty white shirt who took the first shot at Rob.

He was about half a mile away from the rest area and couldn't hear anything being said, but it was obvious what was happening when a female came running from the buildings of the rest area and started hugging one of the two men laying on the ground, obviously hysterical and out of control. *You dumb bastard,* Rob thought of the man. *You should have just stayed in the rest area and left me alone.* Rob couldn't tell if either man was dead but knew if they weren't they would be soon. Without medical care, the bullet wounds would become infected and the person would still die, it would just take longer for them to expire. Rob felt no remorse, knowing the world now operated under new rules. It was all about survival. Either you did whatever you needed to do to stay alive, or you fell victim to someone who would.

Rob drank some water from his canteen then used it to fill the water pouch back up. He was down to the water in the pouch and the water in the plastic water bottle he collected from the ravine. After watching for fifteen minutes, finishing two of the protein bars, and seeing no sign of anyone trying to follow, Rob decided it was time to get going. He looked at his watch. 5:21 pm. Rob secured the .22 rifle to the backpack then jumped out of the truck bed.

As he made his way to the front of the business something caught his eye. *That's an early 60's Corvette. And it looks like it's in pretty good shape. Wouldn't that be something if I could drive that home. Monica would be surprised as all hell when I power slid into the driveway in that.* Rob walked over to the baby blue classic car and found the interior was in great shape, but when he walked around to the hood his spirits fell. The front grill was missing, and Rob could see the engine compartment was empty. *They must have been in the middle of working on the engine. Guess that means no cruising home for me.*

Rob left the car behind and walked out to the front gate. He once again threw his bag over, this time using the paracord attached to the carry handle to lower it to the ground, then followed it and stepped out to the street, checking his surrounding the entire way. As he looked around, Rob could see a side street just east of where he was standing so he moved close enough to read the street sign. Avenue G. It was time to head into the city.

Yucaipa had a population of around 50,000 people and covered an area of twenty-seven square miles. Not as densely populated as Moreno Valley but not as rural as San Timoteo and Live Oak canyons he came through. Rob chose this route due to the availability of cover and concealment but would still need to remain vigilant as he passed through.

Avenue G was a narrow road that curved back and forth along the south side of the canyon as it made its way east for almost two miles where it ended at California Street. It was lined with trees and in several places pushed directly up against the canyon wall and there were numerous houses and side streets Rob would need to navigate past as he followed Avenue G. The side streets came from the top of the canyon rim and turned sharply east along the canyon wall as they descended into the canyon, then turned north until they reached the north wall of the canyon where they turned sharply west and climbed up the canyon wall to the north rim.

There was also a large flood canal that ran roughly parallel to Avenue G but was situated closer to the north wall of the canyon, making its way all the way past California and then past the east edge of the city. Rob would have elected to use that instead of the street, but with the heavy rains it was currently a swollen river.

As Rob started walking east on Avenue G the first thing he passed was another mobile home park on his left, this one completely burned down. On impulse Rob walked into the park and looked around as he walked through ash and the scent of smoke. It was depressing.

Amongst the charred remains of the homes were the belongings of residents who had made a hasty retreat, trying to escape the inferno. Here were some children's toys and stuff animals, apparently dropped as the family ran. There a small SUV with the cargo hatch standing open that had a pile of soot covered clothing and shoes inside. In one burned out shell of a mobile home Rob thought he spotted what looked like three bodies; two adult size and one no bigger than a toddler. He couldn't help shedding a few tears as the sight of the small burned body triggered thoughts of his own son Jackson. Rob couldn't find one home left standing, the entire park, including the combination clubhouse and park office, was ashes. Then Rob spotted what looked like the tail of a small plane sticking up from the wreckage of one of the homes. *I wonder if he was flying when the incident happened and crashed here, causing a fire that took everything out. Or if he crashed and the fire happened later and just happened to burn everything down. Either way, I hope a few of these people survived. This is depressing. I gotta get outta here.* With that he cut through the space between two burned down homes and back onto Avenue G.

Rob soon reached the first intersection which is where the canyon walls began. 6th Place went to the left, due north, and 5th Place angled to the right, in a southeast direction, up the incline created by the beginning of the canyon then leading onto the canyon rim. As Rob paused to check all directions of the intersection he thought he heard a motor. After listening for a few seconds, he was sure of it. It sounded like a motorcycle engine and was getting louder, possibly coming from 5th.

Rob quickly ducked into the bushes on the left side of the road and waited as the motor grew closer. Then, it flew by, going at least fifty miles per hour on the narrow road, and quickly fading to the west. In the quick look he got, there was only one rider wearing all black riding a red and white dirt bike. *If I had a bike like that I could be home in ten minutes. I wonder where they're heading.*

Rob waited a few minutes to make sure there were no others coming, and after hearing only birds chirping and leaves rustling in the wind, he headed back out. As he walked he passed houses that ranged from very large to very small, but they were all similar in that they sat on large properties. A lot of the properties he passed were horse or cattle ranches or small farms. *Too bad I have never ridden a horse. I'd steal one and ride home like I was in the Wild West. Hell, it's probably going to be like the wild west before long anyways.*

Rob kept going, pushing past several ranches and houses without seeing or hearing anything. His knees and feet were starting to ache, so he popped some more ibuprofen as he walked. He reached the intersection with 5th Street and repeated the process of checking in each direction before crossing.

Right after crossing 5th, Rob heard yelling up ahead. He

moved into a small stand of trees on the right side of the road and tried to get a visual of what was happening. Rob could see a white house on the other side of the street and thought the yelling might be coming from there.

After a minute or so four teenagers, three white males and one white female, all between fourteen and twenty years old and wearing black clothing, burst out of the front door of the house, arms loaded down with canned food. They almost made it to the front gate when the homeowner chased them out while yelling that they were thieves and needed to drop the food or he would shoot. When the first teen reached the front gate, the homeowner made good on this thret, shooting one of the boys in the back and causing the rest to drop the food they were carrying. They ran for their lives, turning east in the street and disappearing from Rob's view, leaving their wounded friend behind.

The homeowner was now at the front gate and Rob could see he was a white man in his fifties. He was swearing and Rob thought on the verge of tears. A lady, Rob assumed the man's wife, came out of the house. "Why'd you shoot them? Why?" She wailed.

"This is the last of our food," the man replied, almost in shock. "I told them to just leave us alone and move on to someone else. If they took this food, we would be dead in a week." At this point the man broke down sobbing. "I didn't want to do it, why didn't they listen?" His wife was now at his side with her arms around him, crying as well. After a few minutes they picked up the food the teens had dropped and took it back into the house.

Jesus, what kind of world do we live in now that someone has to decide between starving to death and killing a kid over food? Who's in the wrong here? Rob asked himself as the moral dilemma ran through his head. *The kids for stealing the food because they were quite literally starving to death? Or the man who used deadly force to keep the food that belonged to him, so he could stave off starvation for him and his wife just a little longer?* Rob shook his head, unable to come up with an answer to the question. On one hand he didn't blame the kids for trying to survive, and on the other he didn't blame the homeowner for protecting what was his. He knew in the end he would do whatever he had to do to protect and provide for his family, up to and including killing someone.

Rob didn't want the man to come back out and think Rob was with the group of teens who had just tried to steal the food, so he waited another ten minutes to see if the homeowners would come back out before attempting to pass. Rob moved quickly and quietly, keeping an eye out for anyone who might be watching. He continued past the house and walked almost a half mile before he heard crying. As he came around a bend in the road the three teenagers that escaped the gunfire a few minutes prior were sitting next to a tree crying, lamenting their decision to steal food and arguing about going back to check for their friend. They didn't notice Rob until he was almost next to them. All three quieted down and stared at Rob without speaking while huddling closer together, fear and grief on their face.

Rob realized they were probably afraid he was coming to finish what the homeowner had started back at the house, so he said gently, "Hey guys, sorry about your friend. I know it's not what you want to hear but going back for your friend isn't a good idea. He didn't make it and if you go back you might end up getting shot too."

When Rob mentioned their friend was dead all three started crying again. Between sobs the girl started asking Rob questions. "Why did he do that? We just needed some food. I know we shouldn't steal, but our parents are dead, and now our youngest brother too."

Between the girl's words and Rob being able to see the resemblance they all held, he realized they were all siblings. Siblings whose parents, and now youngest brother, were dead. His heart broke for them. "Listen, I'm sorry about your brother and your parents. I don't know what to tell you, other than I'm sorry and you guys need to watch out for each other as much as possible. I know it's not much but take these. Maybe they will help you get through a few more days." Rob pulled the protein bars from his backpack and gave them the remaining ten bars. They looked at him stunned before taking the bars. *Probably the nicest thing anyone has done for them since all of this started.* "You guys live around here?" Rob asked.

The oldest boy answered, "On fifth near Avenue K. Our neighbors wouldn't help us, said they didn't have any food to spare. That's why we started trying to steal it. We have a little food at home, but I knew it would only last us another day maybe, and I wanted to try to make sure we don't go hungry at all. Our parents both had heart problems and when the power went out I think their pace makers stopped working too. And now Jake is dead, and it was all my idea. It's all my fault." He and his remaining siblings broke down sobbing again.

Rob waited for them to quiet back down before speaking. "I can't imagine what you guys are going through, and I won't patronize you and say I understand your pain, because there is no way I could know. What I will tell you is you are doing the right thing by watching out for your siblings. I'm not saying stealing from others is the right idea, but maybe some of those stores on Calimesa on the other side of your house wouldn't miss a few things from their shelves."

The boy blinked a few times and Rob could see the lightbulb go off in his head. "Why didn't I think of that? Stupid, I'm so stupid." He shook his head sadly as he talked.

"You're not stupid, you're learning. This is a whole new world we are living in." Rob wasn't sure why, maybe it was the looks on their faces, maybe it was the thought of his own brother being left dead in someone's yard with no way to bury him, but he offered to do them a favor he never should have considered. "If you want, I'll go back and see if I can get your brother. Like I said, he didn't make it, but I know if it was my brother I would want to properly bury him."

"Really? You'd do that for us?" the girl asked. "Why?"

"Like I said, if it was my brother I wouldn't want to leave him there. No promises, all I can do is try. You guys wait here for me and I'll be back, okay?" They all nodded so Rob turned back around and walked the half mile back to the house where the carnage had taken place. He arrived at the edge of the property and studied the house for a minute as he tried to come up with a plan. Their brother was laying in the front yard on the sidewalk about five feet from the front gate and there was no way Rob would be able to sneak in and carry him out of there without the residents having a good chance of spotting him. *Why did I offer to do this? I'm the stupid one.* Rob decided a direct approach would be best.

He walked right up to the front gate and yelled towards the house, "Hello, anyone home? Please don't shoot, I just need to ask you something!"

"What the hell do you want? Just leave us alone or you'll end up like your friend!" a male voice responded from inside.

"I just want to carry the body away. All those kids are siblings and they would like to properly bury their brother, that's all. I promise I'll just pick him up and be on my way." At mention that the kids were all siblings Rob heard a female burst into sobs from inside the house.

"Why would I allow that? They're the ones that stole from me," the man snapped at Rob.

"You old bastard!" The woman screamed at the man. "You already killed their brother, at least let them mourn him with a funeral!"

"Look, I'm not siding with the kids, "Rob said. "I'm not saying what they did was right, but they have suffered enough. They're just kids, at least let them have some closure."

A few beats later the male finally answered, voice hoarse, "Okay, go ahead, but no funny business."

"No funny business," Rob agreed. He opened and walked through the front gate and approached the body. He could see the kid was about sixteen and had taken a round right in the middle of the back, through his spine and probably into his heart. *Looks like it was instant at least. Small solace.* Rob picked up the body and positioned him into a fireman's carry. "Thank you," Rob said towards the house as he turned and walked out of the gate. He didn't bother trying to close it as he turned and headed back east. He walked the half mile back, pausing once to reposition their brother and once to rest for a minute. As he walked he could feel a wet stickiness begin on his neck. *Damn, I should have used the rain poncho to cover myself. Oh well, too late now. At least he's too young to have any serious diseases. Probably.*

As he was approaching the remaining siblings he could see all three had a despondent look on their faces. He was only a few feet away when the oldest finally looked up and realized Rob was back. He jumped up and helped Rob lower his youngest brother to the ground where all three siblings gathered around and started crying again.

Rob waited respectfully a few feet away to give them time to mourn their dead loved one. Listening to them was heart wrenching. After a few minutes he quietly asked, "Hey guys, I'm really sorry, this might not sound like the right time to ask something like this, but I have to know. Some of his blood got on my neck and back, he doesn't have any STD's or anything like that you know of, right?" All three shook their heads no, so Rob continued, "Okay, thanks. Listen, I'm going to get going now. Again, I'm sorry about your brother. I hope you guys get through this. Good luck to you."

The oldest boy looked at Rob. "Hold up, what's your name?" he said through his tears.

"Rob."

He got up and stuck out his hand to Rob. "Thank you so much. I'm Joey, that's Miriam, my brothers are Johnny and Ricky." His voice cracked as he said the last name and Rob knew Ricky was his dead brother. "Thank you for bringing him back."

"You're welcome," Rob said with a sympathetic smile as he shook Joey's hand. "Good luck to you guys. Take care of yourselves."

Rob turned and walked away. When he was fifty feet down the road he heard Miriam yell at him, "Hey!" Rob turned back around. "Thank you," she said, tears streaming down her face. Rob gave her a sad smile and a little wave before continuing to walk. He said a prayer for the kids, knowing it was probably a futile gesture but doing so anyways. As he walked he took the bandana from his backpack, used a puddle to wet it, and did his best to wipe the blood from his neck and upper back.

Rob arrived at the intersection with 3rd Street. A little east of the intersection on Avenue G he could see a roadblock, made with disabled cars, set up with several men and women standing around, all of them armed with an assortment of firearms. He thought about trying to talk his way through like he did with Jim Bowman in Live Oak Canyon but decided not to. Maybe it was what he just witnessed with the teens, or maybe what occurred on the freeway, or the situation overall, Rob wasn't sure exactly why, but he decided that approaching the roadblock would probably be a mistake. So instead, he turned left and headed north on 3rd. It was sooner than he wanted to turn but would still take him in the general direction of his house. As he walked it started raining again. Not very hard, but enough for Rob to take his rain poncho out and put it back on.

Rob soon arrived at the bridge that took 3rd over the storm runoff canal. He paused and tried to decide what to do. He could take the small service road that ran next to the canal, but he would be next to a lot of backyards the rest of the way up the small canyon and he figured people would be more likely to shoot first and ask questions later if they thought he was trying to sneak around their backyard. And being on the service road would severely restrict his movement if he was confronted with violence as he would have the rushing canal on one side and fenced in backyards on the other. Or he could continue north on 3rd, taking the sharp turn up the north wall of the small canyon. That way would take him into more populated neighborhoods, and possibly more issues to deal with.

After a couple minutes of debate Rob decided to take the canal. California, which is what he would take north from the canyon, was only half a mile due east, and with the rain he was hopeful he could make it through without being spotted. He turned east once more and started trekking through the mud of the service road, keeping an eye out for anyone that decided they didn't want him walking near their backyards. Rob could see the canal had several feet of fast moving water in it. *That was some storm, I've never seen the water level this high. Definitely can't escape that way if something happens.* Rob could see the clouds were still thick and black, heavy with rain, and the rain that had turned into mist and back into a steady rain didn't appear to be letting up anytime soon. *Probably going to rain for the next few days. Hopefully not like it did earlier before I make it home.*

Rob was only about fifty feet from 3rd when he heard another motor. *Sounds like another dirt bike.* A quick look around revealed nowhere for Rob to hide. On his left was a six-foot wooden fence surrounding a backyard and on the right was the raging storm canal. His only option was to hunker down and hope for the best. Rob drew his gun in case he needed it, turned back towards 3rd, and then crouched down next to the wooden fence to reduce his profile.

The engine grew steadily louder before it suddenly appeared. It looked like the same rider Rob had seen earlier, wearing all black and riding a red and white dirt bike, but this time they weren't alone. There was another bike behind the first, this one blue and white, but with the rider also wearing all black. They were moving fast, coming down 3rd from the top of the north ridge of the canyon. *They better slow down or they'll never make the turn at the bottom, especially with all this water on the road.*

Rob's prediction proved correct. The first bike, the red and white one, didn't slow enough to negotiate the sharp turn and the rider ended up dropping the bike and bailing off. The bike slid off the road and into the dirt shoulder before colliding with a wooden mailbox and stopping, with the rider sliding into the suddenly stopped bike. The rider on the second bike, the blue and white one, could see what happened to the first bike and slowed just enough and was able to barely keep control of the dirt bike.

The downed rider got up with some difficulty and Rob could see them limping. They walked in a circle for a minute trying to walk off the injury before going back to the dirt bike to assess the damage. By this time the second rider was off their bike and running up to the first. Rob could see a quick discussion being held, and while he couldn't hear what was being said it was easy to see the second rider was trying to assess injuries on the first rider, but the first rider was insisting they were okay.

After a few seconds of arguing both turned their attention to the dirt bike. With a little difficulty they righted the bike and checked it over, looking for any obvious damage. Once the riders were satisfied with their check the uninjured one got onto the bike and tried to start it. It took several tries, and what sounded like more than a few curse words, before the bike suddenly started. The engine sputtered several times before suddenly roaring to life, but even then, it sounded off to Rob, like it wasn't running quite right. The rider on the damaged bike pointed to their own bike, obviously telling the injured rider to get on the blue and white dirt bike. At first there was resistance, but after several more points and a raised voice from the uninjured rider, the injured rider limped over and climbed onto the undamaged dirt bike. After several tries the bike finally started and both riders rode away, this time at a much slower speed, south on 3rd.

That's interesting, thought Rob as he checked his watch. 7:19 pm. Due to the cloud cover it was already darker than the last two nights, especially with the clouds blocking out the aurora that shined and turned night into twilight. *I wonder what they're doing. Scouting for new places to loot? Scouting for mobs that are moving towards their houses? Just out joy riding and risking their lives in the process?* With no way to answer the questions, Rob stood up, happy to have not been spotted, and started walking east again. He was one third of the way to California St when he heard a voice. "Hey, what are you doing? Best not be tryin' to get in my yard."

Rob turned to find the source of the voice. An older black man, probably in his seventies, and holding a gun and flashlight was standing on his back porch glaring at Rob. The house was set at the bottom of the canyon walls with the front driveway making the steep climb up to the street on the opposite side of the house where Rob now stood. "Just walking through sir." Rob tried to sound as respectful as possible.

"Walking where?" the man asked, voice ripe with suspicion.

"Home, up off California and E." Rob gave one of the major intersections near his house.

"You sure you ain't back here looking for places to loot?" he asked sharply.

"No sir. I've walked all the way from Riverside, just trying to get home to my family."

"Riverside? Shit that's a long ways. Everywhere else you see like this too? Without power I mean," the man asked.

"Everywhere I've been through its been the same. No power, no working cars, nothing," Rob replied.

"Shit," the man thought for a minute. "Okay, I guess you're good to go. Just keep walking though. I might be old, but I can still drive a tack at twenty-five yards with my 1911 here, even in the dark" the man said while giving his gun a little shake at his side.

"I got no doubt about that. Thank you for not shooting first. Good luck to you sir," Rob said with a wave and respectful nod.

"And to you, young man," the man nodded back.

Rob made it to the end of the service road and could see California where it swept up the canyon walls and headed north. This street was much wider than any of the other roads that travelled through the canyon. While the other roads were at most one lane in each direction with a line in the middle, California had two wide lanes in each direction with room to park against each curb.

At the top of the ridge where California turned north there was another roadblock, this time utilizing not just cars, but several wooden barriers that were built in place across the roadway. This one kept people from coming south into the canyon area. *Probably part of the same group with the roadblock over on Avenue G. They probably have one on the other side of the canyon keeping people from coming north on California from the south side of the city.* There was no way to go around, it was either backtrack or go through. *Well, they're keeping people out, not in, right?* Rob could also see that the handful of people manning the road-block weren't very disciplined. They were all talking, two were outright laughing loudly, and at least half had their flashlights continuously on, giving away their positions, destroying their night vision, and wasting battery power.

Rob moved up into the street and approached the roadblock from behind. He coughed a few times to make sure he had their attention, so he wouldn't startle them as he walked up. Someone coming up from the "wrong" side of the roadblock got a reaction. "What the hell?" a short thin white man in his fifties carrying an AR-15 said, bewilderment in his voice. "Where did you come from? You aren't from our neighborhood."

"You're right, I'm not. I'm just walking through trying to get home," Rob replied.

"Did they let you through on the other side? They aren't supposed to do that." The bewilderment had been replaced by something akin to irritation.

Rob shook his head, "No, they didn't let me through. You guys have a weak spot."

"What do you mean, weak spot?" the man asked, clearly offended Rob would have the gall to question his neighborhood's security arrangement.

"You know that dirt service road that runs next to the storm canal?" Rob got a nod. "It runs all the way through to the far end near Calimesa. It's wide open, no one covering it. I came up from 3rd."

"3rd Street?" Rob nodded and could see the man's mind racing before he realized what Rob was saying. "Oh man, that is not good. Roger is not going to be happy that was overlooked." He turned to a young teenager in his group. "Go tell Roger about the service road, he needs to address it right away." The teen didn't reply but jumped onto his bike and pedaled away as fast as he could. *They are using them as runners. That's pretty damn smart. Good way to pass info as quick as possible when needed,* Rob thought. The man continued, "Well, I guess you are good to pass through. I'm supposed to keep people out, nothing about keeping people in."

"Hey before I go, have you seen those dirt bikes riding through the canyon?" Rob was hoping to get any information he could.

"Yeah, what about 'em?" the man asked suspiciously.

"I've seen them twice, once down at the bottom of Avenue G when I first turned off Calimesa Blvd, and the second just a little bit ago. One wrecked coming down 3rd headed south. There was another one and they were able to get the first one up and continue on. The bike sounded a little damaged but was rideable, and they took off. I'm just wondering who they were. They a threat? They just with you guys scouting around? Just trying to figure out what I might have to deal with in the future."

"Okay, I guess that makes sense. We don't know who they are. Every day they ride by the barricades a couple times. At first, I thought they were scouting our setup here, but we haven't had any issues with them, so I'm not sure. Now I kinda think they're just kids out joy riding, but who knows?" the man shrugged.

"Okay, thanks for the info. I'll head out then," Rob said as he gave the man a nod and passed through the barrier. The man didn't respond so Rob just walked away and approached the intersection of California and Wildwood Canyon Road.

On the northeast corner of the intersection was a gas station. Rob could see two people sitting on lawn chairs in front of the doors. He immediately recognized them as the owners of the business. Joe Campbell and his son Joe Campbell Jr, who went by his initials, JC. Rob only knew them in passing from stopping there for gas a few times per month, but they were always friendly, both always had big smiles and were always in a good mood. JC was a spitting image of his father, white around five-foot seven and one hundred eighty pounds, brown hair and green eyes, and save for Joe's older looks, they could have been brothers.

After checking his watch, 8:01 pm, Rob decided to stop and say hello. He was so close to home it was a hard decision to make, but knew a friendly visit now could pay off in the long run. As Rob approached, walking through the parking lot and passing the gas pumps, he noticed both men had Ruger Mini-30 rifles, one propped against the wall next to Joe and one laying across JC's lap.

Rob greeted them when he was close enough to be heard without raising his voice, "Hey Joe, JC, how you guys doing?"

JC responded with a nod, Joe responded with a question, "Hey, Rick, right?"

Rob smiled, not at all offended by the mistake. "Rob."

"Sorry about that, Rob," Joe said as he stood and shook Rob's hand with his usual smile.

"No worries. I'm surprised you were that close. I know you got a lot of customers and remembering us all would be quite the feat," Rob said. "So, how's it going around here?"

"Not too bad considering. So far we haven't had any widespread rioting or looting. Everything we have heard of is small time stuff, small groups hitting one or two houses on a street then leaving. Most of the smaller stores in town haven't been hit as most are being protected by their owners, like me and JC here," Joe waved his hand towards his son before continuing. "The big grocery stores have all been emptied out though. I think Yucaipa is doing a little better than most of the surrounding areas. At least that's what I gather from the ham radio."

The mention of the radio got Rob excited and his questions came out in a rush "You have a ham?" Joe nodded. "What have you been hearing? What's it like in the cities? Is the blackout widespread? Or just southern California? Or the whole country or world? You hear anything about the military or government trying to help out? What about news from Arizona? How about-"

"Hold up, hold up. Slow it down speed racer," Joe interrupted, laughing.

"Sorry," Rob said, chuckling but a little embarrassed. "I felt like a kid in a candy store for a second. I was at work in Riverside when the EMP hit. I walked through Moreno Valley, San Tim and Live Oak, then up Avenue G to here. I met a few people, but no one has heard anything from anywhere else, except for the emergency message the feds were broadcasting."

"Damn, that's a hike," Joe said with a touch of admiration in his voice. "I'm surprised you made it that far without being ambushed. I power up the ham every six or eight hours and listen, but there is so much being transmitted it's hard to make out what's going on. The little I've been able to gather is that the entire world was hit, nowhere was spared. The big cities are complete chaos, gangs and whatnot taking over. No word from the government other than that emergency broadcast, but if you ask me I wouldn't hold my breath on any assistance from them. That's the short of the long of what I've heard. I did hear that several dozen planes all along the final approach into Palm Springs, Ontario, and LAX all went down and caused some serious damage to places in the Low Desert, the Inland Empire, and into LA." The areas Joe mentioned were regions within southern California, each encompassing numerous cities and population centers.

Rob took a moment to process what Joe said, then asked, "Nothing from Arizona? My family lives in Sierra Vista, down past Tucson near the border." Rob didn't really expect any news but asked anyway.

"Not that I've heard," Joe said shaking his head. "Like I said, the airwaves have been cluttered with stuff. It's hard to figure it all out. But if I do hear anything I'll be sure to let you know if I see you again."

"I appreciate that man, thanks," Rob said. "Hey, you guys still taking cash for supplies?"

Joe shared a conspiratorial smile with JC before saying to Rob, "Me and you both know cash is completely useless in our new society here."

"Preppers?" Rob asked him, asking Joe straight out if he was one of the few in America who prepared for end of the world type scenarios.

"Something like that. And if I had to bet, I'd say you are set up yourself," Joe said while pointing at Rob's chest.

"Something like that," Rob confirmed without saying too much. "So, what will you take for payment now?"

Joe's answer was predictable, "Food, ammo, some jewelry maybe. Anything that has real world value."

"Yeah that makes sense. Hey, if you don't mind me asking, how do you have a working ham? Wouldn't the EMP fry it, especially since it was hooked up to an antenna?" Rob was genuinely puzzled.

"Oh yeah. And it certainly did. It even melted the wire running from the antenna to the ham. Fried the radio itself too. We had a spare ham ready to go for a situation like this. Running a new wire and putting up a new antenna was the easy part," Joe answered, obviously proud of their preparations.

"What was the hard part?" Rob wanted to know.

"Not really the hard part but getting power to it. Right now, we're using a generator. Hopefully we can convert that to solar at some point. Gas is going to go bad at some point, and there will be no one left to refine more. At least not in my lifetime. And maybe not even in yours and JC's lifetime."

"Yeah that's true I guess." Rob decided he had spent enough time there. "Thanks for the chat Joe. I'm gonna take off, I gotta get home." Rob stuck out his hand and shook Joe's hand.

"Thanks for stopping by, it's good to see friendly faces. If you need anything, me and JC will be here," Joe said while waving his hand towards his son.

"Sounds good to me. I'll see you guys around," Rob said. He gave JC a wave then turned and walked back through the parking lot.

As he approached the street he tried to decide which route to take while he checked his surroundings. *I can go straight through on California, but there are those two trailer parks on the left that are always having issues with all the drug dealers and stuff. Or I can cut up to Bryant and go around. Less houses that way but it will add on a little time.* Rob decided to take Bryant Street. He was anxious to get home but wanted to get home in one piece, so he turned and headed east once more, this time on Wildwood Canyon. He made it to Bryant, passing several houses and empty cars stopped into the roadway without incident, then turned left on Bryant to head north.

The first street Rob reached was Sunlight Drive, a T-intersection that went to his right, and checked the street. He was glad he did. Five houses up Sunlight from the intersection was a group of nine or ten people all in their twenties and all carrying flashlights and weapons. Mostly bats and poles, but Rob thought he could see a couple guns as well, but it was hard to tell in the darkness. He stopped and watched discreetly as the group walked up to the house. They didn't bother to knock, just kicked open the front door and rushed in, with several going around the back. *Holy shit, it's a group of looters, and not even a mile from my house.*

With that, Rob took off at a jog. Seeing the group enter the house that way shook him. *What if they've already hit my house?* The only thing that kept him from breaking into a sprint was knowing he wouldn't make it home if he tried to run the whole way, so he settled for a fast jog.

Even though he knew it was reckless he didn't bother checking cross streets anymore, and it almost cost him his life. Vineyard Street was a T-intersection that went to Rob's left. He was on the right side of the street and didn't notice the small roadblock set back about fifty feet off Bryant. The first he realized he was in trouble was a single gunshot and his backpack being jerked on his back. Instinctively he knew someone had just taken a shot at him and hit his bag, so Rob immediately turned to the right and sprinted into the open field, trying to reach one of the few trees that were about a hundred feet ahead.

Rob zig-zagged as he ran, hoping to throw off the aim of the shooter. Just before he reached the tree he heard another shot and some of the bark on the tree shattered. Rob dove behind the tree and tried to catch his breath. He drew his gun and tried to listen in case the shooter tried to sneak up on him from around the tree. *Seriously? I am the dumbest dude alive. Almost home and getting shot at, all due to my negligence. How would that look? Ninety-nine percent of the way there and get taken out just because my patience has run out. Stupid, stupid, stupid.*

Rob was breathing easier, so he stood up and tried to peak around the tree without giving himself away. He could see the roadblock but couldn't see any shooters. *Where are they at? They waiting behind the cars for me to take off again?* Another couple of minutes and still nothing moving that Rob could see. *I gotta make a move, I can't just sit here the rest of my life, however short that might be. They could be trying to flank me and the longer I stay here the more likely it is they'll succeed if they do.*

Rob turned and studied the house behind him. The tree he was behind was technically in the front yard of the house which was set back several hundred feet from the roadway and didn't have a fence around it. *If I angle just right I can keep the tree between me and the roadblock and make it to the corner of the house. Then dash north across the open area to that next tree. I should be just about out of their line of sight if they stay at the roadblock. Only problem is I'll be in the front yards of these houses. But I guess I don't have a choice. Face the certain danger of the shooter at the roadblock? Or the potential danger of someone who might be in one of the houses?*

Decision made, Rob first studied the houses for any movement or light. Seeing none he faced the direction of the roadblock and walked backwards, careful to keep the tree between him and the shooter. Rob reached the corner of the house and moved around the side, then sighed with relief. *That was close. Just one more move and then I'll be good.*

As he was getting ready to move Rob heard something from the direction of the roadblock. It sounded like someone tripped and fell, a few curse words, then another person telling to first to be quiet. *Two of them. This is not good. Maybe I can get the drop on them.* Rob took his backpack off and left it on the ground next to the house. He quickly but quietly moved to the rear of the house, then around to the other side, stopping at the corner to make sure the people trying to shoot him didn't have the same idea, then circled back to the front of the house.

Rob peeked around the corner to the front side of the house and found nothing. *They probably found my backpack.* He moved down the front of the house and arrived at the corner, then slowly looked and found two people. One was crouched down over Rob's backpack with the other standing, holding an AR-15, and looking towards the back of the house.

Staying next to the house in case he needed to use it for cover, Rob aimed his gun at the one with the rifle and activated his pistol mounted light, at the same time saying in a commanding voice, "Drop the gun, put your hands up. I won't say it twice." Rob could see both individuals were average build, and both were wearing all black clothing with ski masks and gloves.

The one crouching immediately put his hands in the air as he slowly stood up. The one with the rifle hesitated for a moment then quickly spun around, moving the barrel of the rifle in the direction he believed Rob was standing. Rob fired twice, hitting the man once in his left shoulder, the other in the side of his neck. He dropped to the ground, dead before he even started falling. By this time the other one was standing, eyes closed, and repeating "Please don't shoot, please don't shoot me," over and over as his bladder lost control and flooded his pants.

"Turn away from me, take five steps, then go down to your knees. If you do anything I don't like, you die like your friend. Understand?" Rob asked.

"Yes," the guy replied, voice quivering with fear.

As soon as the guy turned away Rob knelt next to the man he just killed and did a very fast search. *I have to hurry, they might have friends coming to investigate the shots.* He found a thirty round AR-15 magazine and a cheap pocket knife. Rob put the magazine into his own pocket, left the pocket knife, and approached the other individual. "Don't move. You have anything on you?" Rob asked. The guy shook his head no, so Rob continued, "I'm going to give you a quick pat down. I swear to you, if you even breathe wrong I will kill you." Keeping the gun trained on the man's back, Rob gave him a quick pat down with one hand and found nothing interesting. As he was checking, Rob asked the man, "Anyone else back there at the roadblock?"

The man shook his head no and Rob gave him a small push on the back of his head, "I want to hear it. Anyone back there?"

"No. We were manning the roadblock when we saw you walk by. We have the overnight duty, everyone else is asleep," he answered, on the verge of a break down.

"Okay. Keep doing what I tell you and you'll live to see another day. Go all the way to the ground and count slowly to five hundred. Then you can get up and go back home. Don't so much as twitch until you're done counting. Understand?"

"I do, yes," the man's voice now sounded more relieved than scared as he went fully prone.

Rob quickly retrieved his backpack and put it on then picked up the AR-15 rifle that was lying on the ground next to the man Rob had killed. From the time Rob shot the first man, to the time he put on his pack, was less than ninety seconds. He walked back to the front of the house and checked back towards the roadblock. He believed the man when he said there was no one else, but Rob wasn't taking any more chances. *Time to go.*

He took a couple deep breaths then ran flat out, faster than he ever had in his life, north through the open area. *Nothing like being shot at to turn me into an instant track star,* Rob thought wryly. Several houses in a row were set far back off the road with no fencing around the front of the properties so he ran straight through without stopping. As he approached the last open property he angled back towards the street. By this time, he was huffing and puffing, chest burning, heart feeling like it was going to explode, but because there was no cover to provide somewhere to rest, Rob pushed through the pain. When he reached the street, he slowed and studied the area behind him towards the roadblock. Satisfied no one was following he turned and kept jogging.

Rob had learned his lesson, and the last T-intersection he

crossed before reaching the street he would turn down, he checked thoroughly before crossing. He jogged until he reached Eureka Avenue where he turned left. Halfway down on the left was his cul-de-sac. Now he started to run again, not able to hold himself back any longer. As he ran he couldn't think of anything except his family. Question after question ran through his head. What would he find when he reached his street? What would he find at his neighbor's houses? What would he find at his own house? Would his wife and son be there? Would they be injured or worse? Would Matt be there? Would his neighbors be there? Would Rob find the neighborhood burned down, or the houses looted with no survivors?

What felt like ten lifetimes but was only a minute or so passed before he reached his own street of Oday Court. He made the left turn and almost ran right into another roadblock made of more disabled cars, one of which was the SUV his wife drove. A powerful flashlight was shined into Rob's face and he immediately stopped and threw his hands up to block the light. The roadblock was manned by two of his neighbors, Josh Henderson, a twenty-nine-year-old white man that stood six feet tall and weighed a solid 220, and Jose Carmona, a thirty-five-year-old Latino from El Salvador standing five feet eight inches and weighing 180 pounds. They both recognized Rob immediately, lowered their flashlights, and greeted him with huge grins. "Rob it's good to see you man" and "Hey compadre, how you doing?"

Rob almost ignored them but stopped. "Hey guys, my family?" he asked, not even caring about being almost blinded with their lights.

Josh answered with a smile, "At your house buddy."

"Thanks, I'll catch up with you guys." Rob sprinted to his house. It was the second one in a set of five tract homes that were built on the left side and the end of the cul-de-sac. On the right side of the street was the backyard of a large property that faced Eureka, and the rear parking lot of a large church that faced California. Rob ran up to his front door while fishing the house key from his coin pocket. He got to the door and tried the knob. Locked of course. He stuck the key in and started knocking at the same time. "Monica! Monica! I'm home!" he yelled out to his wife. He didn't have a chance to turn the key before the door flew open and Monica jumped into his arms.

She burst into tears, "Oh my God, I can't believe you made it home. I've been so worried."

"I know baby," Rob said with tears in his own eyes. "But I did. We are together now, everything is going to be fine now." They both knew it wasn't true. Nothing was going to be fine now that the world had changed so dramatically, but it didn't matter. They had each other, and that was the most important thing of all.

After a long kiss they both stepped into the house. Rob dropped his backpack and the AR-15 by the front door and walked into the living room where he could see Jackson laying on the couch. Being careful not to transfer any of the dirt, blood, and grime Rob had picked up on the way home to his son, Rob picked him up. "Hey little buddy, Daddy's home. I missed you." Jackson smiled as Rob gave him a kiss on the forehead. Rob felt Monica walk up and put her arms around both him and Jackson. Nothing had ever felt so good.

He looked at his watch. 9:19 pm. He was home.

EPILOGUE

The coronal mass ejection spewed from the sun forty six hours earlier had left no part of the planet untouched. Every city in every country was now without basic utilities or transportation. It was just less than two days since the power went out and the world was already spiraling out of control. Ironically, the places least affected by the EMP were areas considered uncivilized or barbaric by western civilization standards.

The world population was about 7.5 billion and so far, over the last two days, the number of births had just about kept pace with the number of deaths, keeping the world population more or less stable. However, this was just the beginning. Over the next few days, months, and even years, the world population would fall, and fall drastically. The loss of life would be somewhere between seventy and ninety percent. The first to die were those like the ones Rob seen in the burned out mobile home, or the lady in the flipped over car. The next to die would be those with medical conditions that required daily or weekly care, such as people with pace makers or in need of dialysis. Next would be the old, the very young, and the disabled that had no one to care for them. Then it would be those who were unable to obtain clean water or extra food, and those who were preyed upon by their neighbors.

During this time, disasters both natural and manmade would continue to occur. As a result of no power, nuclear power plants would soon run out of backup power and would be unable to keep their fuel rods cool. This would result in meltdowns and render large areas uninhabitable for years. Dams would no longer be maintained and would eventually fail, releasing trillions of gallons of water and flooding large areas. Hurricanes and snow storms would continue to dump rain and snow, but now there would be no forecast to warn people to evacuate or prepare for the worst. With no real medical system people would be at risk of death for ailments that were easy to treat prior to the EMP. Diseases like typhoid and measles would return. The flu would be a deadly threat again. Major surgeries would no longer be possible. Even the death rate of newborn babies would skyrocket.

Few would survive the first few weeks and months. Even fewer would survive the first few years. Humanity's only hope of survival would be for enough humans to survive long enough to start rebuilding and repopulating the earth. However, enough had to survive the catastrophe unleashed by the sun first.

ABOUT THE AUTHOR

Pat Riot has twelve years Law Enforcement experience, the first five in a volunteer capacity, and the last seven as a dispatcher. He loves fishing, hiking, the beach, target shooting, and of course spending as much time with his family as possible. He grew up in Southern California and currently lives there with his wife and two sons.

Made in the USA
Coppell, TX
16 August 2024

36014024R00132